PLANTATION SHADOWS

MALA NAIDOO

Naidoo, Mala

Title: *Plantation Shadows*

Print ISBN: 978-0-6455450-5-0

Ebook ISBN : 978-0-6455450-4-3

ABOUT THE AUTHOR

Mala Naidoo is an Australian author. She has worked as an educator in Australia, and in South Africa during the grip of apartheid atrocities, and the early days of its dismantling. Mala Naidoo upholds *justice for all* in her novels, short stories and poems on culture, race, gender, and identity. Her writing mission is: *in our angst and joy we are ONE under the Sky of Humanity*

For ancestoral courage in paving the way
forward... against all odds...

for truth is truth, to the end of reckoning.

—**William Shakespeare**

Measure for Measure

CONTENTS

PART ONE

MILLY

Stout, sinewy jointed sugar stalks struggled to rise above ever widening cracks on dry earth, unsure where to point a finger at generational shadows.

EDGAR TOOK my secret to his grave. My mother's silence was my living death.

MY GRANDPARENTS ARRIVED in South Africa as a contingent of indentured labourers to toil in the sugar fields of Natal.

Destined for enslavement in a low-paying life— what choice did they have? Poverty or a chance for change, a better life, perhaps?

My father was fortunate. He wrangled the role of

assistant manager to the sugar plantation owner, Albert Sherman, who treated him almost as his equal. No person of colour had this privilege that my father secured—he smoked cigars, drank the finest whiskey, and laughed with Albert Sherman on his front porch late on balmy, mosquito-infested Sunday nights. My father boasted to all living creatures that the Shermans were *his* adopted family. He was singular in all he said and did. I knew no extended family—we lived a nuclear, insulated life on the sugar plantation. My father was an only child. That was all he ever said about his childhood. For migrants who came out in droves from colonised countries to the sugar plantations—the paperwork was shoddy. No accurate record of lineage, left us rootless. Our family of five, my parents, two brothers and I, was the sum of our ancestry.

I was the youngest.

There was a three-year gap between me and my second brother George and five years to my eldest brother, James. We lived at the rear of the sugar plantation with rolling sugar cane fields between our home and the Sherman household.

My parents had no say in naming their children. As a young married couple, they arrived on Sherman's Sugar Estate, bright-eyed that the future would bring freedom from past shadows. My siblings and I were born on the sugar estate. Albert Sherman arranged all our christenings at the local church in Umgeni, the town closest to the plantation. He elected himself my godfather and gave the three of us names that stamped our identities. James, George, and Milly. Albert Sherman truncated my name from Mildred to Milly. He was the father of Henry and Thomas. Albert's wife died during Thomas' birth. For many years, I heard whispers of her *long and difficult labour* without understanding what it meant.

My brothers had a private tutor in Maths and English as Albert Sherman's gracious offer to educate them in what he considered necessary. I attended a small school in Umgeni. We were taught by European teachers, and locum teachers from our community. School authorities bussed plantation children to school. The only bus stop was on the main road, a long walk through dusty footpaths. When my father had saved enough of his paltry earnings, he paid Albert Sherman for one of his beat-up vans. From that point on, Edgar transported me to the bus stop every morning. He was my father's all-purpose helper, from gardener and house cleaner, to taxi service transporting me to the bus pickup point when my father was busy.

My brothers were allowed to play games with Henry and Thomas. I had one friend on the plantation. Albert Sherman's helper's daughter. He employed Edgar's wife, Norah, as a nanny, cook and house cleaner after his wife died. Norah raised Thomas from the cradle. Edgar and Norah had a daughter, Siyabonga. Siya and I were close friends.

Albert insisted on the name Siya, and she enjoyed the shortening of her name. We maintained our friendship through the many trials and tribulations of our lives. Siya died two years ago.

My earliest memory of living on the sugar plantation was of heat, dust, flies, and sleepless nights in combat with mosquitoes. Our simple wood and iron home had an outside bath and toilet. When I say bath, it was a bucket and hosepipe in a makeshift enclosed space. Every morning at 4 am, my mother heated water on our coal stove. She washed our clothes on a large stone and hung them in front of our kitchen door. Her hands were rough and calloused from the work she did. When Albert Sherman needed extra hands to clear sugar cane for the mill, my father would tell my mother to go out into the field. She carried a basket on her back and wore a tattered straw hat while she toiled in the heat and dust on Sherman's Sugar Estate. My father condemned the riots that indentured labourers engaged in two years after the first ships came in from the East. Their gripe was the poor working conditions and pay.

'What ingrates our brothers were to riot and demand!' he would rant. All he saw was his privilege as he genuflected to Albert Sherman's gleaming boots. When my brothers were teenagers, they had to assist on the canefields after school. Never me. James and George teased me for being Albert Sherman's pet.

'Silly Milly, the boss man's filly,' they would sing, chasing me around our small backyard.

Edgar shook his head when he heard them. 'No James, no George, be kind to your baby sister.'

My father enjoyed the banter. Never once did he chide my brothers for teasing me. I hated the taunts. My mother said nothing, but her eyes empathised with me.

Siya was my confidant.

'Let it be, Milly. These boys and men think they are funny. Laugh it off.'

'It hurts that my brothers do this to me. You are lucky not to have siblings.'

Edgar and I never spoke about the teasing, it was enough for me to hear him tell them to stop their unnecessary behaviour.

Edgar was a good father to his only daughter.

When we were younger, I witnessed his delight upon seeing Siya when Norah walked over with his lunch. They sat together under the pecan trees in the garden, sharing his lunch. I watched them from our front porch. When Norah and Siya said their goodbyes each day, Edgar would lift Siya into his arms and hug her.

'You be a good girl now; I'll see you at dinner time, ready to tell you a bedtime story I made up.'

Norah held Siya's hand on their return walk to Albert Sherman's home.

I watched them and yearned to be loved like Siya.

My mother did as she was told. If she displayed affection, she was mocked and had to suffer my father's bad temper.

I was a lonely child with no sisters to share my highs and lows.

School holidays were by far the worst. I counted the days when school would open. Siya and I could only see each other on Sundays at church. In this strange land of divide and rule, and a master and servant mentality, it was gratifying to note that under God's roof, black and white prayed together as the plantation population—even though we sat in segregated sections of the church. Albert Sherman and his family and associates took up the front seats of the church. We sat in the back row, with an empty row separating them from us.

I wanted a career, independence, and freedom to choose whom I associated with and where I went.

When Siya left school, I heard demands from my father for me to do the same.

His caustic tone was always the same. 'Perhaps we should send Milly back to our village. She will make a fine match there. It will stop her foolish dreams of a career and independence.'

My mother whispered, 'How can we send her back to the village after what happened to me?'

I spent most of my life pondering what my mother meant. What happened to her we were not privy to as a family.

We never had after dinner family conversations on the old days of my parent's lives. My father was cold and austere. I wondered whether he was always that way, or perhaps Albert Sherman's persona rubbed off on him. He grovelled to Albert Sherman, telling my mother to prepare spicy meals for his boss.

'Romola, add extra spice to the Rogan Josh. Mr Sherman loves a curry that makes him perspire.' He laughed and thumped the kitchen table.

Informality did not mar his apparent closeness to Albert Sherman. 'Mr Sherman' was always just that to my father. My mother did her expected chores in silence, dutifully cooking whatever he demanded of her.

'I do so enjoy watching him devour the meals you prepare, and after he has had a good feed, I get to have quite a few drinks with him.'

I promised myself I would never grovel to Albert Sherman or his sons. Never. My father's sickening laugh, and boastful claim to being an expert at *currying favour* with the boss, irked me.

My last two years of high school were challenging. I argued with my brothers, who were the spokespersons for my father's decisions in my life.

I did not want to marry before I had a career.

Things did not quite work out the way I desired.

A stream of men, of varying ages, family of other plantation workers, arrived as prospective suitors. I received no invitation to the discussions and meetings with those unsuitable choices. All I had to do was show up dressed like I was already a bride. My mother's gold bangles, off-limits to me in my younger years, adorned my wrists, making me their prized tagged livestock.

Up for the biggest bidder.

My mother knew my inner struggle with this, but begged me to comply.

'Please Milly, don't be difficult. Give this one a chance. Don't make your father angry. It affects our relationship.'

My mother was an expert at concealing her marital woes. Did she hope her non-existent 'relationship' with my father might improve? How could she live this way? I could never live such a life.

I had to parade as if I was a contestant in a beauty pageant, and made to feel guilty for messing up my parent's marriage.

There was no love lost between them, and the known secret that my mother ignored was my father's relationship with the widow, Mrs Biswas, from the neighbouring plantation. I sensed their secret connection whenever they were in church. The skin on the back of my neck grew hot and fine hairs pricked up like antennae guiding my quick head turn to catch my father's wandering eye. Kesha, the schoolyard gossip, confirmed his longstanding infidelity.

'Do you have stepsisters and brothers from Mrs Biswas?'

She said nothing more. Left me confused and anxious that my father might leave us. My mother had no means to self-sufficiency without him. I questioned her, but she told me to stop spreading the gossip I heard.

Her body language confirmed Kesha's suggestion. I don't know if I have other siblings. Today, at this ripe old age, I'm none the wiser, except for the silent hurt my mother endured. One Christmas, the back of my father's van was loaded with a fir tree and bulging boxes of gift-wrapped parcels. The tree and laden boxes never appeared in our home.

My demanding father and compliant mother dictated my life. As a teenager, I thought of them as a match made in hell. I could never question my mother on why she accepted such a life for fear of the outcome from my father. My mother's allegiance to a man who wronged her on every count baffled me. I let my imagination run wild, creating situations between them that empowered her. The one that disturbed me was the image of the Goddess Kali I saw hanging in Kesha's family home. Kali of my imagination bore my mother's face, and her victim, my father's contorted face and curled body under her bright hennaed feet. Her raised eyebrows, wide-eyed stare, and spinning trident raised above her head, made her formidable. This image gave my mother the strength I perceived she needed. She locked the extent of her hardship in her soul.

I weathered the hot, dry, and humid days at Sherman's Estate and later lived there with my husband—a man, hand-picked by my father and accepted by my mother. The strident men in our family drowned our voices. James hid his softer nature during his growing-up years.

At seventeen, I realised that the inner strength my mother bore belied her meek outward expression. To have mothered a boy like George took grit. My father fed George's ego, making him aggressive towards my mother and me. He shaped George in his image. To have a husband and son exploit her patience, treating her like a doormat, put a raging fire in her belly in how she shielded me against outside forces.

One Saturday night when my father and brothers were out carousing, my mother and I heard a loud banging at our front door. My mother locked me in my bedroom and told me to stay under my bed in case of gunfire. She grabbed the garden fork from the back veranda, and my father's whiplash from behind the kitchen door.

She called out in a loud, harsh voice, as I had never heard before.

'Who is there? I have a gun. I will shoot. Leave now if you want to live!'

Raucous laughter followed. I heard stomping footsteps pass by my bedroom window.

Slurred voices sounded as drunk as my father's after a night out with the boys, or whenever he spent a Sunday evening with Albert Sherman.

The impatient banging and kicking on our front grew louder. I wanted to run out to help my mother, but she locked me in. After a loud thud, the lounge window crashed to the floor with the deafening force from kicks of iron-tipped boots. Whacking sounds and screams seemed to go on forever. Then silence. Dead silence.

My mother let me out of my room and shoved me into the pantry.

'Sailors! Sailors!' She shouted. 'They want you. Stay there. Don't move.'

A menacing booming voice penetrated the silence. My mother was unprotected. The front door was down. The chilling angry voice yelled, 'Where is your daughter? Where is she?'

A rapid cracking sound, followed by wailing cries for mercy, terrified me. My mother dashed to the pantry, pulled me out, and told me to run with her through the sugarfields to Albert Sherman's house.

We ran without shoes, tripping along the way, panting and gasping.

Once we crossed the clearing to Sherman's homestead, my mother rushed to Edgar's quarters and yelled with the air she had left in her lungs.

'Edgar! Edgar! Open, please. They want Milly!'

Edgar flung open the door and told Norah and Siya to stay indoors.

'Mrs Romola, what has happened? Who did this? Come inside. You both must sit down and have some water. Norah, come quickly, bring some warm water and clean towels, please.'

On our fearful flight across the sugarfields, my mother and I did not feel the the cuts to our feet and knees. Blood dripped out of our wounds.

My mother begged Edgar not to report the matter to Albert Sherman.

'Mrs Romola, we must tell baas Albert there was an attack on his property. He will notify the police. You and Milly are not safe.'

Norah told my mother the police had to be brought in, as she and Siya were also at risk of a similar attack.

This made a dent in my mother's refusal to involve Albert Sherman and the police. She feared my father's rage when he realised others had to be called in to protect us. His odd values were his neglect on one hand, and the mask of pretence that made him the super protector of his family.

The police arrived, and escorted us back to our house. The bloodied scene on the front porch spoke of violence and perhaps death. One soldier lay groaning at the bottom of the porch steps. The other six my mother mentioned were nowhere to be seen. The police said that a ship had docked at the harbour the day before and late-night drunken revelry led them to our door.

The carnage before me made my mother a reincarnation of Kali. Her supreme power destroyed evil or frightened it away in her manifestation of maternal strength.

Albert Sherman's reaction worried me.

He was kind and concerned, offering to take my mother and me to the hospital.

'Where is your husband, Romola?' Albert Sherman's words silenced the police officers as they waited for my mother's response.

'I'm not sure, sir. He took George and James with him.'

'That is bloody irresponsible to leave you both alone at night.'

'We don't mind, sir. We are used to it.'

My mother's voice quivered as she looked at me for confirmation. I nodded in agreement.

'Don't protect him. He must answer for why one boy was not with you tonight. You were brave and strong tonight, Romola. These sailors were powerless against you because they were drunk. We need security here to protect you. More ships are coming in during this time of year, and once the word gets out about how you fought off the men, others might try to do the same to test you or seek revenge for their mates. Too many days tossing on the high seas makes these fellows soft in the head.'

Edgar and a few of the plantation workers cleaned up the porch.

When my father arrived with George and James, Albert Sherman told them to go to bed and that he would see them early the next morning.

What transpired between him, my father and brothers, was never revealed to my mother and I.

It passed as if it had never happened. Albert Sherman posted two security guards at the front of our home every evening from 6 pm to 6 am.

My father remained mute on the matter.

MY HUSBAND, Chiddy, was fifteen years my senior.

It's not just the fifteen-year gap—Chiddy was much older in every way.

He had a gentle face and manner, but rarely engaged in conversation. I accepted Chiddy as the man I would marry because my mother was ill with worry about my future. Did I agree for me or her?

Albert Sherman held my wedding on his private section of the estate. A gigantic marquee went up on his sprawling two-acre front lawn. Tables and chairs set in clusters of ten, seven clusters of seated strangers. I only knew my immediate family and Chiddy's three siblings. His parents died years before our marriage. He distanced himself from his siblings, which shut them out of my life. Albert Sherman's motivation was to have all his relatives and friends at my wedding, to show me off as his prized godchild—of colour.

I overheard a woman say, 'You are very good to these people, Albert. Other plantation owners should take a lesson from you.'

Albert Sherman smiled, nodding. 'It is the only way to get the most work out of them. They are hard-working by nature, and if you throw in a few things like this, there's much to gain. The bride's mother cooked this delicious wedding feast.'

'Aren't you lucky! The food is scrumptious, better than any oriental restaurant I've ever tried, and I have travelled far and wide, as you know.'

'Perhaps you should mention that to the bride's parents, they might gift us many more such meals, or come over and cook in your home. They do love to please.'

My skin crawled hearing this. It made us faceless, shameless, and grovelling.

My long-suffering mother had to cook on my wedding day to entertain Albert Sherman's guests. She was happy that I was married. It meant lessening her hardship with my father and the cultural freeing of the burden of having an unmarried daughter.

Like my mother, I settled into a life of serving, and caring, cooking and cleaning. Chiddy and I lived in my parents' adjoining wood and iron cottage. Edgar helped both our households.

Seven months later, my daughter Sugar was born.

Albert Sherman insisted on naming my baby. It felt like he was naming a pony he had purchased. I registered Sugar as Rosalind. Nobody knew her as Rosalind. My mother told everyone I went into early labour because I was overly active, a tomboy in all I did! All Chiddy said at Sugar's birth was, 'Good, good. Lovely, lovely.'

Three years after Sugar, Zola was born. Chiddy served Albert Sherman as loyally as my father did, and Albert Sherman took it upon himself to also name our second daughter.

My girls were as different as night and day. My mother said Sugar looked like her northern Indian ancestry. Sugar was as white as the driven snow, but had my eyes, not my personality. Albert Sherman said she was so white she could be mistaken for one of his children. Sugar lived in the clouds. She preferred reading and writing. Zola was a cut-out of Chiddy, in looks and her strong, silent manner.

My mother died when Zola turned two and Mrs Biswas moved into my parent's home. Six months after she passed. George and James moved out of our plantation home, refusing to refer to Mrs Biswas as their mother. I kept away from the family home as much as possible.

Chiddy was a good father, distant like my father, but he provided for his family first. Our lives were mapped for us. I did not love him, but took great care of him, like the devoted wife I was schooled to become. We had nothing in common.

I enjoyed knowing about the world outside the plantation and listening to music. All he did was work, sleep, and work more. My birthdays went unnoticed. Birthday celebrations were reserved for Sugar and Zola.

Our few conversations were around the children—what they needed and how they were performing at school. Each time, he said, 'Good, good. Lovely, lovely.'

I never complained, except to Siya. She married her high school sweetheart and moved off the plantation to settle in Zululand. We wrote letters to each other sharing some of our innermost secrets and met when she came to the sugar plantation to see her parents.

Be happy Milly, Chiddy is a good man. You will grow to love him.

Most of Siya's letters reminded me to be grateful I was lucky to be married to Chiddy. I did not agree. I felt cheated of sharing my life with a man of my choice—a man I did not have to *grow* to love! The younger me could not understand how love grew if no root existed.

Siya's mother continued to take care of the Sherman household, well into old age. Thomas Sherman ensured Norah had good care when she was frail. He employed a young woman to assist her. She was the only mother he knew. He spoke fluent Zulu, played the piano, and wrote poetry against the rising tide of racial inequality. His father never accepted that his son was not cut out for plantation work. Henry was Albert Sherman's golden son. He toiled the land, supported his father's decisions, and his father prepared him as the successor to his booming sugar business. Siya revealed the arguments in the Sherman household after Albert had too many drinks.

'What's the matter with you, Thomas? You daydream all the time. Use your hands to earn your adulthood. Look at Henry, soon he will take over the business if you don't pull your weight around here.'

Siya said Thomas never retaliated, and her mother intervened on his behalf.

'Aye, no, baas, Master Thomas is still young. Give him some time.'

'Hey Norah, you keep out of this. You spoilt the lad. I have a good mind of telling you to pack your bags and to go back to your village, but Edgar is a good man. He will leave if I do that.'

Every family has its internal politics, as we did when Mrs Biswas moved into my mother's bedroom. My father and brothers argued over her arrival. It grew from a low, spluttering flame to where my father, one day, threatened George with a cane cutter. George was a hot head, a bully like my father. James kept a cool head and planned his exit rather than having words. One night he snuck out, leaving our family, and George followed him the next day.

My father relied on Chiddy thereafter. My father's

friend, my husband, became my father's son.

———

THINGS RAN SMOOTHLY until Sugar was a teenager. She was a wild one, not like Zola who avoided trouble. Sugar enjoyed the lifestyle on the white side of town where she had a few girlfriends. They did not know she was from the dark side of the plantation. I don't know what story she spun, but she was an expert at fabricating things. This is where she and the pragmatic Zola were different.

The first time Sugar was in trouble, the police came to the house to question Chiddy. I had no say. Women had to shut their mouths, or face the embarrassment of the police telling us to be quiet. The gloved fist thumping on the front door rattled the windows. Sugar got home an hour before they arrived.

'Open the door, Chiddy! Where is your daughter?'

Chiddy was a fierce protector of our family.

He opened the door with a blank stare. 'I have two daughters, officer. Which one are you looking for, and why?'

'Don't pretend Chiddy, you know which one.'

Chiddy motioned to me to bring the girls out.

'Here they are, officer. Both were asleep.'

'I'm warning you, Chiddy, you better watch this one.' He pointed at Sugar. 'She will put you in jail soon, running around town, like a...' he stopped himself when I stepped forward, my eyes bulging, my hands on my hips, now the Kali of my imagination.

Sugar invited trouble, but no police officer could disgrace her under my roof without proof.

Chiddy went directly to bed when the officers left. I sent Zola to bed and asked Sugar to sit down. She owed us an explanation of why the police were watching her.

'Cut the lies, Sugar, tell me where you were tonight. Your father turns a blind eye to everything you do, but I want to know where you were tonight?'

Sugar frowned, glared at me, and remained silent.

'Speak up, girl, I don't have all night.'

'Why must you always know where I've been? I'm eighteen, so what's the problem, ma?'

'Cheek! That's what you have. Eighteen and living under my roof means you owe me an explanation for tonight. Speak up.'

'I went to an eighteenth birthday party?'

'Where? In white town?'

'You have the answer, so why ask, ma? Come on, I'm exhausted, as are you, let's go to bed and forget about this.'

'Forget about this? You could end up in jail if you carry on this way. There is talk that racial segregation will be legalised, and you try to challenge that? The police are powerful and all they see is black and white. Never forget that!'

'I do what I enjoy, now what are you going to do? Marry me off as your father did to you.'

'That might be the only way to shorten that long tail you've grown.'

Sugar stood up. Her eyes flashing with anger.

'Was your long tail shortened too when you married pa?'

'Go to bed, think about your behaviour and be prepared for the husband we find for you.'

She stormed off with a final retort, 'I'll find a husband for myself. Thank you very much!'

Those words troubled me. Whom would Sugar choose for a husband? She knew there would be consequences if she pursued an interracial relationship. Nobody of colour could dice with the escalating change.

Zola protected her sister by being the keeper of her secrets. To have a sibling's loyalty is enviable. My brothers never knew my secrets because they revelled in my troubles. I was grateful for the bond my daughters shared.

'Don't stress about Sugar, ma,' Zola called out as I passed her room. 'She is sensible, even though she pretends she's not. You raised her, so how bad can she be?'

Zola had a wise head on her young shoulders, but she gave me more credit than I deserved. Her sudden bravery in speaking up for her sister surprised me. Sugar's argumentative manner stemmed from proving that she belonged in two worlds, at home and in the cruel world outside. Her looks made her the focus of judgement. Many suitors approached Chiddy for her hand. Deep down, he knew Sugar had a will nobody could tame.

Growing up on Sherman's Sugar Estate held no excitement. School friends did not want to visit, and my parents refused to let me see friends outside the estate. Siya and I clung to each other on Sundays, and she wrote notes during the week and had Edgar bring them to me.

On rare occasions, preceding the years of us beginning school, when I saw Siya having lunch with her father under the pecan trees, Edgar would invite me to come over when I stood shyly on the front porch watching them. Their lives felt warm and joyous. Simplicity and acceptance of a humble life made them peaceful.

No competition, no aspirations, just happiness to be alive and together. My bond with Siya began during her brief early lunchtime journeys across the plantation to our backyard.

As a teenager, she confided in me about the boys that caught her eye.

'Milly, surely there must be a boy you like. Let out the secret!'

'There's no one. The boys I know are irritating and have big egos.'

'But you will tell me when your heart flutters, right?'

'Sure.' The hollowness of my lie made me uneasy. I could never tell her for whom my heart danced.

When Siya told me she was marrying Zondi, I knew she made the right choice. They were well-suited. He had an outgoing personality and worked in a coal mining office in the Orange Free State. They met when Siya worked at the mining office as a filing clerk. Albert Sherman arranged the position for her. Six months later, they were married. When Siya spoke of having children, she rolled her eyes and laughed, 'It gives me great joy in knowing that Albert Sherman will never have a say in naming my childern. Zondi won't allow it.'

I was not so lucky. I was living in Sherman's Sugar Estate when my children were born.

Zondi's work colleague, Maxwell, liked me. I knew that such a relationship would cross too many boundaries. My father was the one I feared the most.

'Just date Maxwell, Milly, no strings. Keep it a secret. That will be exciting. I can be the decoy as he is Zondi's friend. Your father will never know, trust me. Enjoy this time of your life.'

'I can't do this, Siya.'

'When we visit my parents, I'm bringing Maxwell along so that he grows on you.'

'No, I do not want this, not now, not anytime. I am going to remain single. Look at what my mother had to endure and the pain of knowing there was a third wheel in her relationship.'

'You are far too negative. Give love a chance, my friend.'

Siya let it be, but she dragged Maxwell along to her visits with her parents. He came over a few times and suddenly stopped after his third visit.

Siya said Zondi did not know why Maxwell stopped left his job without telling them. He probably knew there was no hope in hell with me.

George sensed something because he whispered taunts about Maxwell whenever he walked past me.

'Maxwell not here this time with Siya and Zondi? Why?'

I ignored him, but that gave him fuel to go on.

'You don't like him anymore?'

Siya's hope for a romance between Maxwell and me ended.

I completed my schooling at the age of fifteen, but could only do a sewing course through a dressmaker. I had big dreams of being a teacher, but my father said it would do me no good when I married the man he chose for me.

When news arrived that Maxwell was dead, there was talk he was murdered. I felt deeply saddened and guilty for not returning his affection.

Siya tried to comfort me, to no avail.

'You cannot blame yourself if your heart did not feel him. I'm sorry for pushing him on to you. I was selfish in hoping we could have husbands who were also good friends.'

Deep in the marrow of my being, I knew that Maxwell's murder had something to do with his interest in me. That chapter of my life ended with no closure.

THERE WAS great excitement in our home when our granddaughter Candace was born. Chiddy and I were grandparents! Candace, or my Candy girl, as I called her was the centre of my world. She looked nothing like Sugar and every bit like her father, Aru. Chiddy's choice of vocabulary remained stultified on, 'Good, good. Lovely, lovely.' Aru was expressive of his love for his baby girl. He said she was his moon, stars, ocean, and sky. Sugar loved Aru's open nature, so different to her father. Although Sugar and Aru lived a distance away from Sherman's Sugar Estate, I visited her often, especially after Candy was born. Edgar drove me to see my granddaughter whenever I asked.

Candy excelled at school and played the piano with great skill. She entertained us at our family gatherings. An aging Albert Sherman loved her piano playing and invited her over whenever she visited us. Her piano playing gave her privilege in his home. For all the lessons I had from the gracious and generous support from Albert Sherman, I was nowhere near the accomplished pianist Candy proved to be. Albert Sherman bought a second-hand piano and had it delivered to Sugar's home to encourage Candy to keep up her playing.

When Candy left to take up a job offer in Australia, I grieved her departure but supported her decision. She had big dreams and Sugar knew that although she pursued a brief teaching career, her lost opportunities would not recur for Candy.

'Don't be sad ma, she needs to live her dreams. I could have made something more of my life if I had the courage to do what Candace is doing. Trust me, I have no regrets with the wonderful family I have.'

'I know, I am happy for her but selfish in my sadness at her departure.'

'Candace said she would send us tickets to visit once she's settled. That's what keeps me from being sad.'

'Oh, Sugar, how wise you have become from those wild teenage days of yours.'

'Not wild, ma, just wanting freedom. Aru has soft-ened that spirit.'

'As long as he has not killed it!'

We laughed, and I was content that Sugar had reached this point in her life. She was calm, tolerant, and easy to be around. Zola and Sugar shared a wonderful relationship. Each knew the other was always there through their angst and joy. That is all a mother can hope for, that her children will support each other.

Zola, Sugar, and I considered ourselves blessed with Candy's generosity to visit her in Sydney. Our trip to Australia was our first holiday away as mother and daughters. Zola and Sugar insisted I have a glass of wine on the flight from South Africa. I had never put alcohol to my lips before, and nothing would make me do so now. Nothing. Seeing my father swagger home after visiting Albert Sherman on a Sunday evening left me with a lasting impression that it was destructive. I heard my father argue with my mother on the nights he could not hold himself up on his feet. She prepared herself for his drunken behaviour by ensuring I went to bed early. I heard some of their arguments. One of those nights is hard to forget.

'Romola, hey...*bekar*, get up, warm me some food,' he yelled loud enough to wake the dead.

My brothers were either out for the evening or chose not to defend our mother.

'Why do you drink so much? You must stop. It's not good for you.' My mother spoke to him in a soft, tearful voice.

'Leave me to what I enjoy. You had your fun days until I broke Manny's legs to save you from a horrible life.'

I swear, hand over heart, I heard my mother say, 'You killed him.'

My father's response sucked the air from my lungs.

'So, are you sad about that? Look at the life you have and the family I gave you.'

'Enough now, let's go to bed. You will wake Milly.'

'Did you not hear me? I said warm me some food. Or you can cook me some eggs.'

My mother said nothing more. I heard pots tinkling and knew she was serving my father at that ungodly hour. I promised myself I would never marry if this was what married life was like. Her life was a hard and unhappy one. She tried to save me from my father's wrath when she told me I had to marry Chiddy. I'm grateful that Chiddy was not a hard-drinking man. He was distant, but a great provider of life's basic needs. As my daughters grew, they understood that Chiddy and I were in a marriage of convenience.

Before Chiddy, my father arranged a meeting with a young man named Vajin, and his parents. Vajin's father worked on a farm in Umhlali. I had to oblige to take the heat of detection off my heart's truth.

Vajin was lovely, but we both knew from the outset that we were playing to our parents' whims. He wanted to travel, and I wanted to be free to choose who I loved. After the formal introduction, Vajin and I strolled in the garden, away from four sets of listening ears and watchful eyes, to get to know each other.

'Look, Milly, I'm not interested in getting married. How about you? I understand the pressure you must be facing from your parents.'

His bluntness caught me off guard for a second, but relief made me giggle.

'I'm so glad you said that, as I'm not keen to either. My pressure is from my father. My mother has no say.'

'Good. Yes, my ma too does not speak up for fear of angering the old man.'

'What are we going to do about this?'

'Let's play along with their hopes for a while, then tell them we can't marry.'

'What reason are we going to give them? My father pushed for this.'

'I'll take the pressure off you. You can say I already have a girlfriend.'

'Do you? I don't mean to pry. Don't answer if it makes you uncomfortable.'

'You are a good person, Milly. I'm sure something will work out for you. I don't have a girlfriend, but want to work and travel. My parents won't understand that.'

'I know, but I hope it does not bring you trouble.'

'Don't worry about me. Put up with me for a few weeks before we drop our intentions on our parents.'

'I appreciate your honesty. You are a good person, too.'

We made that pact and a warm friendship developed between us.

Many years after Zola was born, I heard Vajin was living with a man in Mauritius. I wish he had told me.

Our brief friendship was lovely, and I would have kept his secret.

If there's one thing I did well, it was to hold a secret tight.

Now when I think back to that time when Vajin and I schemed up a plan, I realise how ludicrous our lives were. Sugar, Candy, and Zola would never have tolerated such a situation. They spoke up and spoke out against patriarchal control. Thankfully, Chiddy and Aru were fathers of a different mindset. Aru was by far the better father. Chiddy was a good man who could not give vent to his emotions. My girls needed fatherly affection. A hug and a kind word go a long way in a child's life.

Chiddy provided and protected like a ward.

I yearned to be loved unconditionally, but doubted that would ever be my claim. Not now. My fleeting years of passion dissolved when I married Chiddy. Edgar knew my heart. For all his struggles as a man with no voice in his native land—he was noble, compassionate and had a heart as big as the Southern, Indian, and Atlantic Oceans. I often wondered what happened to my cryptic scribblings when they disappeared from my wastepaper bin. My mother knew my yearnings, but was silent. I studied her face for a hint of acknowledgement that she threw out my cryptic scribblings, with no success. She hid her whole life in her locked heart and threw the key overboard, mid-sea, en route to South Africa.

Was I, with all my secrets, that different from my mother?

When Candy girl said she was marrying the love of her life and she wanted us to attend her wedding ceremony, I cried for a week, and my daughters scolded me for drowning their joy. Sugar raised Candy with a good head on her shoulders and a heart that guided her choices. When Sugar and I met Terence I felt assured that he laid his love at her feet.

He was attentive, loving in his gestures, and respectful of the work she did. Chiddy suffered a ruptured spleen and could not fly to Australia for Candy's wedding. He left a bulging envelope with money on the kitchen table and said, 'For you, Sugar, Zola and Candace.'

I reached out to touch his arm to thank him, but he had already walked out the kitchen door.

Zola, Sugar, and I shopped for the finest outfits we could find. Aru's niece was a dressmaker. He commissioned her to help us with what we could not find in the limited stores available to us.

THE CELEBRATORY AIR when we arrived as the South African wedding party in Australia was wonderful. We claimed my granddaughter's kitchen as our own and baked the finest homemade biscuits and decadent treats to sweeten the groom's palate.

It's a cultural norm to *sweeten* the groom and his family to seduce them into cherishing our girl. I enjoyed the time spent with Zola and Sugar, baking the goods in Candy girl's large, modern kitchen. There was much laughter in the air. Aru helped us pack everything into air-tight containers. He was involved in his daughter's life from the day she was born.

My Candy girl's wedding was the proudest day of my life. She made a life for herself in a new land without her immediate family and met a wonderful man who worshipped the ground she walked on. Marrying the man she chose would bring her a long and happy life of togetherness. Regarding romance, I think of myself as one who has lived through joy and sadness, and I cherish true love when I see it.

A multicultural wedding, in an explosion of vivid colours, had love floating in the air like a heady fusion of hot spices. This union was a match every couple desired. Candy girl wore a silk gown with diamanté stones stitched along the bodice.

With her swept-up hair, and curly wisps hanging on the nape of her neck and forehead, she looked exquisite! Her accentuated high cheekbones, added a regal air to her aura. She looked angelic! Sugar, Zola, and I brimmed with pride. I could never understand why joyous occasions made me tearful. I sobbed with joy and sadness.

My mother steeled her emotions behind a hard veneer. I never saw her cry but don't doubt it might have happened behind her closed bedroom door—the bedroom my father rarely slept in.

The thing I noticed on the wedding day was Candy girl's in-laws' behaviour. They cast a suspicious eye on Sugar and whispered among themselves. I did not let it worry me. My granddaughter was happy. It shone through her eyes like the sparkling diamanté stones on her wedding dress.

I developed the ability to perceive judgemental behaviour from a young age. It nudged my shoulder or the back of my head to turn or look up at what generated negative energy. Second sight is a curse. It left me uneasy and unsure of how I could act to ease the signals that came to me. Are we born with this, or does it develop because we live in the shadows of shame?

We returned to South Africa a week after the wedding, exhilarated and proud of Candy. I did not imagine that our pride and joy would be shattered.

Five years after Candy girl's memorable wedding day, she was upset with me.

For all that my life has been, I naively did not predict that I would have to answer for what seemed illogical in our family. It's the burden of responsibility of being the last trusted surviving member of a generation, to bring clarity to a family. My brothers, well, George, in fact, held questionable truths. Nobody turned to him. I had to ensure that I won my grand-daughter's affection again. She is my greatest pride and joy. If she was upset with me, then it made sense that Sugar would be too. I could not allow this to happen. Whatever the problem is, I promised myself I would solve it—if it was within my power to do so.

PERFECTION IS A DESIRE, not a reality.

PART TWO

CANDACE

My name is Candace Laws, Milly's granddaughter, and the only child of Sugar.

I spent a glorious childhood in South Africa with the women in my family, oblivious to the murky waters that ran deep in the blood and bone of our family. I asked a lot of questions as a child and got the same answer from my grandmother.

'We do not know our ancestry. Aren't you happy with the family you have?'

My mother sang the same tune. I stopped asking when I accepted that my future depended on me, not on knowing everything about my closeted family.

I was furious with my mother and my grandmother.

What did they know? Why did they bury it?

My mother had a life of untold privilege as one

with a much lighter complexion than anyone in our family.

Grandma Milly refused to entertain questions about how my mother got away with travelling on *Whites Only*, public transport, and how she had a few white girlfriends.

Grandpa Chiddy, my maternal grandfather, was at least fifteen years older than my grandmother. I hate bringing up skin colour, but he was a striking man with skin that shone under the brilliance of a full moon, and a brilliant smile that melted my heart. He would do anything for my grandmother. Everybody knew he was hopelessly devoted to her. Grandpa Chiddy's silent presence left a gaping hole in our lives when he died. My grandparents had two children, my mother, and her younger sister, Zola, by three years. Zola and my mother were like night and day in more ways than one. They were sisters with only one thing in common, they had my grandmother's brown, almond-shaped eyes. If they had to wear a mask, this feature confirmed their blood ties. As a child, every time I looked in the mirror, I wished I had my mother's skin tone. I looked every bit like my father. He was a good-looking man in his day, a second to none, my mother called him, proud that he was hers. As I grew older, skin tone never bothered me.

Old man Albert Sherman took to naming my mother and her sister. Sugar earned her name from him because of her sugar-white skin. Great-grandfather, an austere man, according to my mother, passed before Albert. He lived under the sad illusion that he was Albert's social equal.

My grandmother shared a few family stories when we gathered during the holidays. She said she wanted to keep them alive among the women in our family because the men cared about nothing but success.

'Candy, you are lucky, my darling, that you did not experience what I had to go through. My father thought he was an Englishman. I had deportment lessons from Mrs Knott, but she thought I was hopeless because I slouched. The pressure was on me, not my brothers, to emulate not just British manners, but more British aristocratic ways. I had to eat with fine cutlery, and my mother would have to report to my father on the progress of my ladylike manners. Perhaps he hoped I would curtsy to him. My horrible brothers spent every waking moment mocking me.'

'How did your father afford such luxuries for you? His earnings would have been basic as a sugar plantation manager. Am I right, grandma?'

'Absolutely! Albert Sherman funded all the extras to assimilate me, and later, attempted to do the same with your mother, not so much Zola.'

'Control freak! Now I understand why you are so different from the grandparents my friends had.'

'Yes, it was as though I had two lives. I secretly named Albert, *Sugarman*. It made me feel I could dissolve his effect on our family. Technically, he was a Sugar-daddy!'

Although we kept it light-hearted, I felt grandma Milly's sadness. Her freedom snatched from her. She could not be *her* person. I tried asking her how my mother could have white privilege when no one else did. Her evasiveness was annoying, and my mother adopted the attitude that nobody questioned her, and that she would not throw away any chance for a dangerous taste of a good life.

On one hand, grandma Milly was the fountain of knowledge on her father's behaviour, but not on anything racial or political. I often contemplated why she made no direct comments against racial inequality. It affected her like the rest of us, yet she kept her thoughts private.

My mother left the plantation when she married my father. For all her white privilege, she married within the expectation of adherence to race. I suppose she could not legally escape the law if she married a white man. It was not possible. The Immorality Act prohibited interracial marriage. My mother would have faced imprisonment if she broke that law. She was a much sought after irresistible woman. A stunning catch for any guy of any race! Yet she married Aru, the son of grandpa Chiddy's friend—it was her choice.

I had a happy childhood and loved visiting my grandparents at the sugar plantation. The stories grandma Milly shared about Mrs Biswas conveyed her disappointment in how her father treated her mother.

Why did he do it? *Sugarman* Sherman must have sanctioned it. My great-grandfather never went against Sherman's expectations.

Living outside the sugar plantation fuelled my understanding of the damaging impact of racism. The plantation existed in a bubble. Three races lived on the vast estate, in separate quarters. Each was respectful of the other, but forced into a social alienation that makes no sense other than upholding power and control.

The sugar industry had privilege—its financial growth boomed under the indentured scheme.

The Shermans were among the wealthiest of sugar estate owners. My great-grandfather remained on the estate until his death in dutiful service to Albert and his son Henry.

How was it possible that my great-grandparents arrived in South Africa as first-generation migrants with no ties to the land of their birth?

Grandparents of friends had family ties in the old country. We were unique. This left me thinking there had to be a dark secret that my great-grandparents held close. My mother protested that she knew nothing. What did she care? She tried to forge a new identity with no success.

Grandma Milly said great-grandmother, Romola, told her their family were from the north of their homeland, hence the lighter skin tones. None of this made any sense to me, and as I grew older, it did not interest me. All I wanted was to live in Australia. As a child, I had a pen pal in Perth, and that sowed my desire. I focused on upskilling as much as I could and applied for every job I could find in Australia. My grandmother tried to talk me into working in South Africa.

'You will meet a handsome young man, have babies, and be near us. Family is important, Candy. We need family.'

I knew grandma Milly felt her mother's lack of family as a disconnection from her old life growing up in another country. There was no way I was going to throw away my dream. I marked Australia as my home.

After securing a job in Sydney, I began living my dream. My tiny apartment in Newtown was perfect for me. Living on the brink of the city hub, I worked hard, and achieved much in a brief space of time as a charted accountant.

I married a wonderful man.

I met Terence, a promising surgeon, at a friend's housewarming party. He was Doreen's husband's best mate. She worked in the first company that employed me in Sydney. Soon she became a close friend. My mother said it made her happy knowing I had a sister-friend. She worried about me being an only child. Before Doreen married Nate, she visited my mother and grandmother in South Africa. The racial mistreatment in the land disturbed her. She spent hours chatting with grandma Milly about her thoughts and feelings about living in racial pockets. Grandma Milly was the worst person to engage on that topic. She was a fence sitter on anything pertaining to race matters. Doreen did not antagonise or push for more. We chatted at great length about the plight the country faced.

'Please excuse grandma Milly's nonchalance. She has been this way for as long as I remember.'

'Part of me understands her, not wanting to talk about what grieves her.'

Little did I realise that Doreen's words would ring true.

My mother and grandmother visited Terence and me before we got married. He accompanied me to South Africa once, and said he confronted the source of his ancestry on that visit.

My mother and grandma Milly adore Terence. He is also an only child.

Both sides waited anxiously for a grandchild. We wanted to wait until we had a spacious home and could afford to have me stay at home to raise a family.

When Terence's mother and grandmother visited us, they were inquisitive about my background. When they met my mother, his grandmother asked, 'Is your family of mixed-race?'

'No, not mixed-race, but our ancestry is from northern India.'

She narrowed her eyes, and I felt nervous.

'That can't be right, your mama has white blood. I saw the spidery veins in her cheeks. Our family is black, down to our roots. I cannot see how your mama can be without white blood.'

At our wedding, Terence's grandmother spoke to anyone who would listen to her about how strange she thought it was that my mother looked different to the rest of our family.

Back then, I did not expect the troubles to come.

I RAN my tax services business for five years. When I had a reliable manager in place, Terence and I tried for a baby. As luck would have it, I was pregnant after two months of timing my most fertile part of the month. We decided to visit my parents and grandmother to tell them the news they had waited a long time to hear.

Terence's mum promised she would not share our news until my mother and grandmother knew a baby was on the way.

We waited for three months until I felt safe travelling on a long-haul flight. Our stay was a brief one. My grandmother was upset that she could not have more time with us.

We gathered in the lounge room of my parent's home, after our welcome home dinner. Grandma Milly and aunt Zola looked anxious.

Terence spoke first. 'Family, Candace and I are here to see you for a special reason.'

The whispers around the lounge room made me smile. Grandma Milly said, 'Are you both moving to South Africa? Then, I can die with a smile.'

'Ma!' my mother chastised in her well-known commanding tone. She disliked my grandma's morbid conversations about her death. She did it often, and my mother always made her annoyance heard.

'We are all going to die someday, so what's the harm in me expressing what will make me happy now?'

Terence laughed and slapped his thighs.

'Grandma Milly, you will die smiling, not soon, however you will smile for many years when we give you our news.'

Silence sat on every heavy head and stooped shoulder in anticipation of what news awaited them.

Terence gave me a wink to break our good news.

'We had to tell you all face-to-face that we are expecting a baby!'

My mother shrieked with delight in typical Sugar style, and my father hugged me through tears and shook Terence's hand.

Grandma Milly looked anxious. She stared at me

with unblinking eyes for a minute, lost somewhere behind her frozen look.

'Ma, are you ok?' Aunt Zola asked and got no response.

'Grandma, are you speechless with joy?'

'Yes, yes, I am,' she whispered. 'Forgive me. The news took me by surprise. I am overjoyed. Grandpa Chiddy would have loved this news. Come, let me hug you both.'

My emotional grandmother's strange unemotional reaction troubled me.

My mother asked if we were having a boy or a girl. I told her that would remain a surprise until our baby was born.

We spent a wonderful week staying a few days on the plantation with my grandmother and a few days with my parents before we headed back to Sydney. On our flight home, I asked Terence what he thought of grandma Milly's reaction.

'She was subdued, not at all as I expected. I wonder what has come over her. It must be age, that is the best answer, I think. Don't stress over it. Your mum's reaction was great. She's ecstatic.'

'You're right, I won't let it worry me.'

With six months to fill my head and heart with dreams about my forthcoming baby, I felt every beat of the precious life within me. A new generation to our family would be here soon.

Nobody could steal my happiness.

My obstetrician advised halting travel in the last two months of my pregnancy. This was an open invitation for my mother to fly over to Sydney to spend three months with us. A month after she arrived, my father followed. He spent a week with us, and they took a holiday around Australia.

My father hugged me before stepping out to their waiting taxi.

'I'm so glad you made this move to Australia, Candace,' he never called me Candy like grandma Milly did. My mother would, on rare occasion refer to me as Candy, but my father carried the air of formality of a true gentleman.

'So am I, and meeting Terence was in my stars!'

Terence laughed, 'Yeah, we carry three countries on our shoulders. Our baby has a rich fusion of cultures.'

'Do we get to know the gender of the baby yet?' My mother searched our faces for telltale signs that we knew.

'No, we are waiting to be surprised when the baby arrives.'

'Come on, Sugar, that waiting taxi is charging us by the minute,' my father touched my mother's arm to hurry her along.

My mother continued to talk with a backward glance at my belly. 'I'm eager because I did not know your gender until your birth.'

'Not long now,' Terence piped in, 'hang in there

and enjoy your holiday. There will be no holidays once this bundle arrives.' Terence patted my belly and put his arm around me as we watched my parents leave.

'I'm going to miss your mum's culinary delights.'

'You need a break from all that sweetness and richness, and ma sure knows how to indulge you!'

When I opened the freezer later that day, a few Tupperware containers stared up at me, clearly labelled, *For Terence*.

My gestational diabetes prevented me from being tempted by my mother's cooking. She made fun of me, saying my name and palate were at loggerheads. I retorted that a healthy child, her grandchild, was important to me and worth any sacrifice. There was much laughter around my mother for as long as I could remember. Nothing dragged her down. She enjoyed being the life and soul of any party.

'I hope your parents extend their stay after the baby arrives. They are good company, and we could use an extra set of arms around here then.'

'As long as you are not salivating about the meals you will receive as the much-loved baby's daddy! Your paunch grows when my mother is around.'

'Yeah, I should take care. I don't want the baby thinking I'm Grandpa Aru!'

Terence knew how to make me laugh. He would be a good father after being abandoned by his father.

We both valued family life.

My parents headed back to South Africa and

planned to return a few weeks before the birth of our baby. Terence and I enjoyed the time alone leading up to our child's arrival. A caesarean birth was confirmed because of the risks associated with my advancing diabetes.

A month before our baby was born, Terence received a request to assist the surgical team in the north.

'I don't think I'll take it on, not so close to our baby's birth.'

'You should go. It is an honour to be called to assist understaffed, struggling communities. Let them know you will come home often in our baby's expected birth week. Dr Tucci will confirm the caesarean delivery date a fortnight before. This will give you ample time to settle in to the position before your paternity leave.'

'You always have a solution to everything! Thank you, that sounds like a good plan. I want my boy to be proud of me.'

'Boy? What do you know that I don't! Now, let's have fun choosing names. I'll choose a boy's name and you can choose a girl's name.'

'Great!' Terence rubbed his hands together, enjoying this idea.

'I have a boy's name in mind. Are you ready to hear it?'

'Yes!'

'Jadon.'

'I love it! Now hear my name if the cherub is a girl.

Deborah. I know it's my mother's middle name. Is that ok with you?'

'That's lovely, Terence. Jadon or Deborah, it shall be.'

'Like you are Candy to your grandma. If our baby is a girl, she'll wind up being called Debbie or Deb. No doubt, Sugar will add in her variations.'

We laughed and shared our visions and wild imaginations of what our child would be like.

'We must raise a confident child that can hold his or her own in the world.' Terence said with a bright-eyed glow.

'And equally, if our child is sensitive, we must allow him or her to be their person.'

'A hundred per cent.'

'My mother said her grandfather ridiculed her uncle James for his tender-hearted ways.'

'I would never do that. You know that?'

'Absolutely. Not after what you went through. You will be the best father for our child. Poor uncle James was a lovely man.'

A WEEK BEFORE THE CAESAREAN, I pulled back from office contact and allowed my team to manage things in my absence. I busied myself with finalising our baby's layette.

I had a restless night on the eve of my caesarean

delivery. Terence could not get away the week before the procedure. Mounting mandatory surgeries needed all hands on deck. Being alone this time made me restless. I lay awake thinking about tomorrow and the days and years ahead. Would I spend many nights alone with the demands of Terence's job?

Calming music did nothing to induce sleep. The caesarean was scheduled for 11 am, and Terence was due home around 8 am.

The obstetrician was eager to proceed because my ankles were swollen, and I waddled around, barely leaving the house. My mother broke her leg during this crucial time. She fell off a ladder while changing a light bulb in the kitchen. The support network I relied on would not arrive on time.

When Terence arrived, I burst into tears.

'What's wrong, love? Are you unwell?'

'I'm so glad to see you. My hormones are all over the place, and I am nervous about this morning.'

'You have the best obstetrician in Dr Tucci. In a matter of hours, it will be over, and our baby will be here. You will feel brand new after the strain your back has endured in recent weeks, is lightened.'

I felt calmer with Terence around, and eager to get to the hospital early. The nursery set and stocked, my bag packed, all I had to do was bring our baby home.

Terence waited to be called to be present at our child's birth. He dashed out for a coffee and got back in the nick of time. Numbed from the waist down and fully alert, I watched my baby arrive in the world. Within minutes of his birth, the nurse placed Jadon across my chest for first contact. Terence sobbed into my shoulder.

'Thank you, baby, he's beautiful!'

We caressed Jadon until the nurse took him away to be cleaned up.

'Dr Tucci says Jadon is going to be a tall boy. He's 3.8 kilograms. That's a good weight. I worried that he would be much bigger because of your gestational diabetes.'

Exhaustion hit me like a sudden summer storm, and I whispered, 'That's good.'

Dr Tucci advised me to remain in the hospital for four days with no visitors for the first two days. My pressure was elevated post-delivery.

After a few failed attempts at getting Jadon latched to my breast, he had his first bottle of formula. I failed at what I most wanted to do, and was awash with tears.

'You are exhausted, my love, don't beat yourself. Jadon feeds off your energy, so you need to rest. The nurses are taking good care of him. I'm checking with them almost hourly.'

'Thank you, you're a good father.'

'A good husband first,' he smiled.

'Is it ok if we don't send any photos of Jadon and me to your mum, grandmother, and my parents for two days? I'm a mess and Jadon is unsettled.'

'You are not a mess, and I will not send photos until you feel it's fine to do so. I will call my mother soon to give her an update, is that ok?'

'Yes, you must talk to her, or she'll think something is wrong.'

'I'll call her now.'

Within five minutes, Terence was back in the ward.

'That was quick. Everything ok?'

'I think it is, but I'm not sure you want to hear what I'm about to tell you.'

'Is your mum upset with me regarding no photographs?'

'That's not it. There was no reply when I called, just a voice message on the other end. My mother and grandmother are on their way to Sydney. I do not know when they left LA.'

I sucked in my breath. 'The house is not ready for visitors? Oh, how will we cope?'

'Leave it to me. You rest and recover. Jadon needs your strength. I'll handle things with our surprise guests.'

I heard his irritation and felt anxious.

Terence's mother made him dance around her demands. His compassion for her as an abandoned wife made it difficult for him to deny her expectations.

His family chose not to forewarn us about their arrival. Their timing was the worst! I wanted undisturbed time to settle Jadon into a routine—not a perpetual happy hour.

When the nurse on duty checked my blood pressure, she called Dr Tucci. My stress levels jumped up a few notches with my in-laws' impending arrival. This meant more time in the hospital if my blood pressure remained high.

Terence's agitation, and my anxiety, affected Jadon —he refused the breast. My baby, fully fed on formula was not how I planned to raise Jadon. I had to calm down. The in-laws would have to take care of themselves.

Terence visited me at seven the next morning. His stooped shoulders, furrowed brow, and creased shirt spelt trouble.

'Wow, you're here early. Did you get any sleep? You look exhausted.'

'Mum and gran arrived last night.'

'What? Did you pick them up from the airport?'

'No, they arrived at our door around 11 pm. They caught a taxi to our place. Bad timing for a surprise!'

'Oh, my goodness! Really? You have slept little, or had no sleep, right?'

'They chatted until 2 am, and I thought it would be rude if I crawled away to bed.'

'You must set new rules for this visit. Jadon needs to adjust when I get home. You have to rest, as do I, while he sleeps. That's just the way it should be.'

Terence shook his head and sighed.

'Yeah, sure. I'll get around to telling them before you come home.'

'Don't leave it too long. It could become their habit because you are on leave. Nip the expectations of late nights today.'

Dr Tucci told Terence I had to wait out the week in hospital. He had to do a few tests to understand why my blood pressure escalated with no visible sign of a problem. I accepted it as my time of rest, and insisted on no visitors, but allowed photographs to be sent around to those closest to us.

Little did I realise that leaving the hospital was walking into a tsunami.

My home underwent rearranging in my absence. Jadon's nursery differed from how I had set it up. His crib sat in our bedroom. His little cupboard moved across the nursery, and his clothes were colour coded in the hanging space and drawers.

A gigantic basket of toys, I did not purchase, filled up a large space in the middle of the room. My irritation had to be subdued.

After the usual pleasantries, I made my unhappiness known about the changes in our home. It fell on deaf ears as Terence and his family cooed over Jadon. Then I heard Terence's grandma whisper loud enough for me to hear.

'The lad has very light skin. Are you sure you're the daddy, Terence?' She guffawed in her smoker's laugh, and Terence ignored her comment. I could say nothing until Terence and I went to bed.

It was the longest day of my life.

Terence sighed and flopped on the bed.

'Being a parent is not easy!'

'I don't need to be reminded! Don't I know it!'

It must have been the annoyance in my voice that made him sit up.

'I don't mean to take away from all you're going through. My family makes being a parent hard work. I'm getting constant reminders about what I need to do.'

'I hear you, but what about your grandma's comment about Jadon's skin colour and whether you are the baby's father?'

He reached for my hand.

'She was messing around, Candace. Please don't over analyse this.'

'I didn't think she was messing around.'

'You must admit, Jadon looks nothing like us. He has your side of the family genes. Jadon is more like your mother, but he has blue eyes and a few light flecks in his wispy hair.'

'Oh my God, I don't believe it! Your grandma has swayed you to accept her ridiculous ideas!'

'Keep it down, please. We don't want my mother and grandma to hear us arguing.'

'The child is not yet a month old, and babies change so much. You know that.'

'I do. Relax and let it go.'

'Did you know your grandma has been going on about my mother's colour from the day they met?

Now she's surmising about Jadon's eyes and skin tone!'

'She's just old school, my love, ignore her.'

Terence made light of what bruised me. He was not prepared to put a lid on it by talking to his grandmother. I had no one to talk to. My mother could not travel for eight weeks. I did not want to call her and tell her about the irritating chatter around Jadon. I promised myself I would let it pass and focus wholly on my baby.

A week later, Terence was called to a meeting, and the wolves cornered me in my home. His mother dished out parenting advice from the minute she saw me. Then, his grandma pushed the forbidden button that afternoon.

'Candace, pardon my asking again, but are you sure your family has no white ancestors? Your baby looks like a white boy. He's got no African American in him.'

'My mother looked the same as a child. All I know is Terence and I are Jadon's parents. We have no interracial ancestral links. I was born in South Africa, and you know what the race laws were like.'

'You sure about that, girl? Historically, laws went unnoticed by some. Is Terence of the same opinion? You should ask him.'

'Please grandma Jess, drop this. This is an unnecessary stirring of nothing which reeks of trouble. I'm just grateful I'm a mama.'

'I don't know that it's nothing, but I'll say no more.'

Not once did she ask how I was recovering after the caesarean, or whether Jadon was sleeping well. My mother-in-law did not stop her mother's judgements.

I sensed trouble in my bones. Grandma Jess was a dog with a bone she would dig up at will. I did not trust that she would stop her speculations.

Terence had the family chat with his grandma and mother. What he asked me after that conversation shocked me to the core.

'This might anger you, but I need clarity, Candace. We must be honest. Grandma Jess makes sense when she says we need to be frank with each other.'

I stood up, ready to react, but paused. With a lowered voice, I said, 'Actually, I don't remember you asking grandma Jess permission to marry me, right? Is she asking you to have a DNA test to prove your paternity?'

'Now that is a good idea, and it will stop her from overthinking the situation.'

'Wow! You want me to do this for your grandmother? What's happened to the man I thought I married? The one no one could sway. I won't allow a DNA test. Your grandmother will not stop. She wants to dig up dirt on my mother. Can't you see that?'

'Don't be ridiculous! Why would she do that or have any reason to? Listen to yourself!'

He walked out of the room, shaking his head.

I was a prisoner in my home, held to ransom by the Laws family, all three of them!

That night, Terence slept on the couch. We avoided each other. I ate dinner in my room, and he spent most of his time away from home. He shortened his paternity leave the week before his family returned to LA. The day they left, he moved out. His last words were that he wanted full disclosure of my family history.

When my mother called, she was worried that I had not responded to her calls.

'What's wrong, Candy, is Jadon unwell?'

Uncontrollable sobs possessed me when she called me Candy.

'Are you getting enough sleep?'

'Jadon is fine, ma. I'm a mess.'

'Talk to me. What's going on? Motherhood in the early days is not easy, so don't feel you have to be perfect at it.'

My mother listened without interrupting.

She sighed. 'This sounds like a replay of my life story. Grandpa Chiddy kept away from his family for the same badgering he underwent from his sisters. What a baffling world we live in! Why is skin colour such an issue?'

'I was glad to see the back of Terence's grandma. His mother commented little, but dished out child-rearing advice every second of the day.'

'I will be with you in a week. Perhaps your father and I can have a chat with Terence.'

'He's moved out, ma.'

'What? When did this happen?'

'The day his family left for LA.'

'Do you know where he's staying?'

'A hotel in the city. I don't know which one, and he's returned to work.'

'Oh dear, this is not good for Jadon, you, and Terence. I'm going to get an earlier flight to Sydney. You need care too after the caesarean.'

'Don't do that. Act on your doctor's advice. Please ask grandma Milly to search into her family history as Terence thinks we are hiding something.'

'I'll try to get her to dig into her memory. She's reticent to talk about this topic as it plagued her younger years.'

In five days, my mother arrived in Sydney.

'Oh Candace, when last did you have a good night's sleep? You must be exhausted. First, let me cook you a nourishing meal. Jadon looks healthy. Have you started breastfeeding him again?'

My mother was garrulous when I wanted a comforting hug. I needed her to take care of Jadon so I could sleep.

'Sleep has been hard, with no help. I'm so glad you're here. I'm near collapse. Jadon is fully bottle-fed as my milk has dwindled, and he has been crying a lot.'

My mother nodded, aware that I had no energy to force Jadon to take to the breast. I wanted to breast-feed Jadon until he was a year old, but life had other plans for me.

After enjoying a hearty lamb roast and vegetables, my mother insisted I go to bed, and she took Jadon to her room.

Tomorrow was the day I would begin probing into our family history.

I slept for twelve hours with no knowledge of how my mother coped with Jadon during the night. Coffee brewing brought me back to reality. Terence was gone. I was a single parent and my mother had to fly to Sydney while recuperating from a broken leg. I was a mess, and I accepted I needed help.

My mother had Jadon in his bassinet in the kitchen while she prepared breakfast. Every so often she looked at him and cooed her love for her grandson. She did not see me at the kitchen entrance when she spoke to Jadon.

'Handsome boy with the bluest eyes. You are innocent in all this. I'm here to get your daddy back. He had no business running off. Naughty daddy.'

'Good morning, ma. Thank you so much for taking care of Jadon last night. I feel refreshed after undisturbed sleep.'

'Good morning, darling, I'm so glad to hear that. Your baby was an angel. He woke twice during the night and had two nappy changes. I wanted to bathe him but thought I would check your schedule for that. Does he have a morning bath?'

'Look at you, you must slow down today, ma. I've been bathing him in the afternoon, although the morning is better. I'm exhausted in the mornings, and have been ever since Terence left. That ruined Jadon's routine.'

'Let me pour you a coffee and we can chat a bit before breakfast and bath time.'

Having my mother home with me was a godsend. I had to tackle our history today.

'We must talk to grandma Milly this afternoon. The longer I leave things, it will put greater distance between Terence and I.'

'I am furious with Terence. It is best we call grandma Milly today. I hope she accepts the serious-ness of the situation and stops that silly secret vow of silence she seems to harbour.'

Counting the hours before we called my grand-mother made me tense. Jadon picked up my mood and fussed throughout the day.

I called South Africa.

Grandma Milly picked up on the fourth ring.

'Candy girl! How are you and my great-grandson and that handsome husband of yours?'

'We are doing ok now that ma is here. How about you? Is aunt Zola spending more time with you while ma is here with me?'

'I'm doing well, darling. She comes over whenever she can. Please send me more photos of Jadon, you, and Terence.'

Grandma Milly did not know that my family life was in tatters and that she held the key to my future. I promised to send more photos and handed the call to my mother.

'Ma, you should have come with me to Sydney. You need to see your great-grandson in the flesh. He is an angel.'

'I wish I could have been there. You rushed over, and I did not have time to get medical clearance to travel. Perhaps if I'm well enough, I could travel with Aru when he comes to meet his grandson. It will be a lovely family reunion again.'

After a few pleasant exchanges, my mother dived into what I needed to know.

'Ma, listen carefully, as you know, Jadon has the palest blue eyes, like no one else in our family. This has caused problems for Candace with Terence and his family.'

'Why, Sugar? It must be a throwback in either his family or ours.'

'Throwback, ma, on our side of the family? How? Terence has moved out of the house, leaving Jadon and Candace alone.'

'What? Why? Does he think the baby is not his?'

'That may well be so. He wants full disclosure of our family's genetic history.'

'You know, I gave him more credit as an intelligent man. This is darn right stupid of him! He must give full genetic history, not us.'

'Ma, stop this, now! I'm your child who looks different, so please, if there is anything you can share with us, please do, for your granddaughter's sake.'

My grandmother broke down. I could hear her sobs.

'I don't have any information. I cannot promise anything, but I will try to go through my family history. My memory is hazy about a lot of things these days. Please tell Candy I'm so sorry this has happened. May I speak to her?'

I refused to speak to my grandmother until she had some answers for me to remove the sword of Damocles. I hated being this way, but I needed grandma Milly to understand the seriousness of my situation with Terence.

My mother and I spent our days chatting about family and enjoying Jadon's antics. Every day he did something new, leaving us laughing and loving him more. Terence loved my mother and had a shred of decency to call her.

'Terence, why did you walk out before resolving matters between you and Candace? Jadon is your child. As he's growing, he is looking more like you. You should come and see for yourself.'

'I can't until Candace gives me something I can believe.'

My mother hung up on him, muttering, 'What an idiot!'

We shared the hope that grandma Milly will have

an answer soon, on the reasons for Jadon's blue eyes. I looked beyond that, to my child's soul—Terence doubted me. Never in my wildest dreams did I expect to find myself in this situation. My mother had to be warned not to be hard on my grandmother. Grandma Milly was fragile in old age. She cried more than I ever remembered at the first sign of unpalatable news.

Terence stayed away from his son, while I waited for information from my grandmother.

I could not still my wandering mind. Much remained unknown in our family. My mother accepted grandma Milly's view that northern ancestry from the Indian continent created shades of brown. Brown—not white. My mother was pale skinned with dark hair and dark eyes. Jadon was the latest family member and the only one with blue eyes, and flecks of golden strands in his wispy hair. As each day passed, his hair grew lighter. I was in a quandary about my ancestry. I wanted full disclosure from Terence on his ancestry, too. Denial from his grandmother, was unacceptable. The Laws family had messed with the wrong girl!

Late one evening, my mother and I chatted while Jadon slept peacefully.

'Ma, please don't get upset with me. I've been pondering on Albert Sherman, who selected grandma Milly as his favourite of great grandfather's children.'

'I don't know where you're going with this, and yes, uncle George teased grandma Milly about that when they were children. It upset her and she spoke about it often to Zola and I.'

'Yeah, I recall hearing that. You don't think Albert...'

'What? Molested my mother, and I'm the product? Never! He was a respectful, God-fearing man. He drank a lot, and great grandfather did the same.'

'Ok, I am only looking at all the possibilities.'

'I am grandpa Chiddy's daughter. Remember that!'

'Sorry, ma, I don't want to hurt you. I'll wait for grandma Milly to investigate.'

'Do you mind if I call aunt Zola and let her know what's going on? This way I can solicit her help in getting your grandmother to hurry things up.'

'Yeah, I have nothing to hide. It might speed up the search for our roots.'

FOR NOW, I accepted I was a single mother.

My mother and I spent many hours, days, and weeks talking about her life in South Africa. She told me why she left the plantation and was grateful that my father refused Albert Sherman's offer to take on a senior position at the sugar estate. An enviable offer that many would have clamoured to accept.

'When I met your father, Albert Sherman tried to rope him into working on the plantation. I hated growing up on Sherman's Sugar Estate. It subjugated us as the white man's possession. Albert Sherman was good to our family, but with race, we had to know our place. His protection of the men in our family gave them enormous heads, and an attitude I'm grateful your father does not have.'

My mother's face was taut when she spoke of that time.

'I tried to shield you from the harrowing experience of feeling like the outsider. That is why your father and I sent you to a private school. We hated doing that, but we wanted you to know the world in a way that living in segregated communities would have denied you. You faced some tough times at the private school, but it made you strong.'

'The bullying was difficult to bear, but I also made some good friends. I appreciate the sacrifices you and pa made to give me a fine education.'

'My father funded most of it. He was a good man.'

'Yeah, I want to talk to grandma Milly about that. Why did grandpa Chiddy give up so much for me?'

'You are his only grandchild. Aunt Zola chose not to marry, and uncle George had countless women, but we heard nothing about him having children. Heaven forbid! They better not come out of the woodwork someday!'

'Uncle George was a bad boy!' We laughed at the antics he got up to, but deep down, I felt the hurt he might have inflicted on many women. When you experience unfair treatment from the one you love and trust, you feel for the sisters going through this hardship.

Our family had so much to celebrate for the successful lives they created in a foreign land. The hardship they endured and survived, but there was much left unsaid that kept us in an impenetrable bubble. I left it all behind when I chose Australia as my home. Little did I think unknown truths would follow me in a twist of fate.

I convinced myself that I would have to seek counselling at some point. I missed Terence, yet I despised what he was putting me through. Why does a man's mask fall off after marriage? It's not like he was *The Phantom of the Opera*! This was to be our lives together, for better or for worse, forever. He created the *worse* with his sudden shift of trust in me. Now his only talent was his self-love! My heart blinded me. I would never have married him if I knew how fickle he could be. I had to raise Jadon to uphold his values with integrity without allowing me, or others that came into his life, to sway his judgement.

———

THE ANTICIPATION of truth is an ulcer waiting to erupt.

PART THREE

EDGAR

I considered myself fortunate to have a steady job to support my wife and daughter. The bonus was that I worked for a family of good people, to me at any rate. There was internal family strife that I was privy to, but I kept my head down and my ears open. My amplified ears were for Milly, and what her father had to say about what was going on at baas Albert Sherman's place. Norah and Siya were under his roof. I went home, down the red, dusty footpath from Milly's house to be with my family on Saturday and Sunday nights. Norah and I joked that the scarcity of our union under these conditions resulted in us having just one child, our beautiful Siya. I cherished my weekends with them.

I lived in the land of my ancestors, but felt I had to earn my right to be here. The segregation laws were rapidly advancing upon us, and I was afraid for Siya, but I was the lucky few with a roof over my head, food on my plate, and some good people around me. I was grateful. Colonialism had stolen the land of my ancestors and our ways. We lived a subjugated existence, but I had my family with me. I could return to them for two hours on weekday nights for our evening meal. What more could a man ask for?

Milly did not have the love Siya had. Watching her grow up a lonely, lost child, made my heart ache. Siya saw Milly on Sundays at church, and I made sure we lingered after the service to give the girls a chance to be together.

I promised Milly's parents that I would bring her home as soon as she and Siya were ready to leave. The problem was telling them when to stop playing, laughing, and talking.

Nobody paid attention to their closeness as children of colour from different race groups. I wished this could be the way for everyone.

It was not to be.

I observed everything that went on in Milly's parents' home and Norah told me about the happenings in baas Albert Sherman's place. There was no privacy between the houses.

Poor Milly was born into a joyless world until her daughters were born. Well, Chiddy was Chiddy—a man of few words, perhaps he had his secrets. That's me surmising, I don't have evidence to qualify this.

Sugar had many arguments with Milly over her

sneaking out some nights when she was home during her school holidays. The police popped by the house to check up on her movements, but she was always one step ahead of them. I wondered how she managed this situation independently, or whether another party was helping her.

Sugar was as secretive as her mother.

Milly was my private concern. No child should ever feel as isolated as she did. I kept a diary. I don't exactly know why I did, but Milly deserved some acknowledgment for why her life turned out the way it did. There had to be compassion and understanding for her situation.

Perhaps my observations and explanations will bring her peace one day.

Milly's heart-wrenching sobs when she thought nobody in the house could hear her made me want to cry for her. I cleaned her room and found her private thoughts in her wastepaper basket. It was not me prying. I had to make sure nothing incriminating got tossed into the bin.

She had a big place in my heart, not only as Siya's best friend, but because I worried about the trouble, she would invite if her father discovered she had mislaid something or exposed a family truth.

Her punishment would be further isolation from the others in the house and no church on Sunday. How does a man think he should punish his child by obstructing her connection to God? Such a man needs to seek supplication for his unholy ways.

You must agree, an ignored child will incline to any attention offered.

It was Siya's sixteenth birthday and Norah arranged a small birthday lunch at our quarters with baas Albert's approval. A few friends from neighbouring plantations arrived by bus, and I picked them up from the bus stop. Milly's father prohibited her from attending. Siya begged Norah to speak to Milly's mother.

'Mrs Romola, please let Milly attend. I promise I will look after her. Siya wants her best friend to celebrate her special birthday with her.'

'I must speak to Milly's father. Please wait while I check with him.'

Norah waited for half an hour until a wan Romola told her that Milly could not attend. Norah asked me to appeal to Milly's father.

The only way I could do this was to seek baas Albert out on the matter.

'What is it, Edgar? Are you planning on leaving us?'

'No baas, I am happy here, and very grateful. I need...'

'Yes, speak up. What do you need? More wages? I can't offer that. I'm sorry.'

'No baas, not money. Can you please ask Milly's father to allow her to attend Siya's birthday party?'

'Is he refusing to send her to the party? Whatever for?'

'Yes, I don't know why. Norah spoke to Milly's mother, and she said her husband refused to give his permission.'

'What the hell is wrong with him? The party is on the estate. It's safe. I'll insist Milly attends.'

'Thank you very much, baas. That will make Siya happy.'

It was a relief to have Albert Sherman address a personal matter. He deserves credit for his kindness to the plantation children. I'm not sure whether my appeal was good, or whether my bowed head, and repetitive use of baas worked. Albert Sherman was a moody man. You never knew which way his switch would turn.

Milly attended. Her joy was priceless.

I had the afternoon off to help Norah with the little party.

Six of Siya's friends made up the small gathering.

Milly's mother baked biscuits and cupcakes during the week. To my surprise, George brought them over on the day of the party. Master Thomas popped his head in at the door, looking for George.

He saw Milly with the girls.

'Was that George? I think I saw him walking over.'

'Yes, he's in the kitchen. I'll tell him you're here.'

Milly knew that Master Thomas would not walk into Norah's and my quarters.

That was the first time Master Thomas addressed Milly directly.

It excited George that Master Thomas came looking for him. They left to play cards on the Sherman porch. Young black and white men had the freedom to associate with each other away from public gaze and judgement. The sugar estate was a somewhat safe place.

Siya had a lovely party and Norah and I were pleased it was possible for her. We had no birthday celebrations in our childhood years.

Poverty could not afford celebrations.

WHEN SIYA TOLD us she wanted to marry Zondi, we were happy for her. He was a good man who had secured a permanent position in the mining office in the Orange Free State. Siya stayed on there as the office receptionist.

She had a traditional wedding lasting three days in my ancestral village. Old and young, childhood friends and relatives celebrated Siya as their princess. A week later, a church blessing in Umgeni gave us another weekend to celebrate Siya and Zondi's union. Norah looked as beautiful as Siya. My two lovely ladies.

I heard rumblings when Zondi's friend Maxwell came over with Siya to visit Milly.

Mrs Romola had the worst of it from Milly's father.

'Why is Zondi's unmarried male friend coming over to the house? The first time I had no issue with it. This is the third time. I don't like the way he looks at Milly. You better stop this before I do.'

'What do you expect me to do? He is Zondi's friend. It has nothing to do with Milly.'

'Where are your eyes, woman? Or are you still blind to your own life before I saved you?'

'Saved me? You stole me.'

'Huh! What are you saying? Do you want to go back?'

Mrs Romola sobbed and did not utter another word. I bled for her.

I gave Norah no details but told her the arguments were increasing in Milly's home.

'Why Edgar? I don't understand. Mrs Romola and Milly are good people. It is very sad when families find unnecessary things to fight over. I will keep them in my prayers.'

Norah was a pious woman. She had a big heart and wanted to help everyone. This is the reason I did not give her the details about the arguments. She would act upon rectifying it, and I feared her anger over the matter would lead to trouble for her. Others cannot solve everything affecting a person's relationship. It was up to the warring parties to make peace with what bothered them.

Too many secrets, that's what I thought—it was sneaking up on them as the years passed.

When George met a girl, he could bring her home for Christmas and Easter and sat next to her in church. There was no marriage contract. He could date. Milly's father could not control George as he would have liked to. I cannot comment too much because I have no sons, but I heard about the issues in baas Albert's home. Norah needed to talk about the things that affected her. Master Thomas was special to her—almost her child.

Baas Albert's issues were with Master Thomas.

MAXWELL DISAPPEARED, and nobody knew why he left.

Three months later, we received news that Maxwell's body floated into a ditch near Dukuza, after a week of unseasonal torrential rain. Police called to talk to Norah and me, and Siya and Zondi. They believed his death occurred somewhere else, and his body either washed down into the ditch or the perpetrator dumped him there. They used the days of heavy rain to go undetected. People huddled at home when relentless rain hit Natal.

There were many drownings over the years as rivers overflowed. The police asked if we knew of any enemies Maxwell might have had. He had an impeccable character and would not have been involved in any criminal activities. I had my suspicion, but kept my mouth shut. The case went no further.

Maxwell was a black man. He had no privilege. Nobody in the legal system cared. If I articulated my suspicion, it would make me a suspect.

When I found a crumpled paper in Milly's bin, I opened it.

My blood ran cold.

Maxwell died because of me. How could they do that to him? He was a good man.

I kept the note in my pocket and hid it in my diary later that night.

If Milly's scribblings got into her father's hands, she would face his and George's wrath. I understood her need to pour out her heart on paper. She had no one to talk to about such things. As much as she was close to Siya, she hid her private matters in her inner tomb. It must have been a troubling time for her. For most of her life, she stayed hidden from view.

The truth has a way of slipping out.

Ears that are not meant to hear it, hear it in the whispers around the house. Bosses must think the helpers are deaf, blind, and stupid, but we know more about each one of them than they realise.

George and James hated their father bringing Mrs Biswas to their home after their mother passed. They looked for ways in which they could blackmail their father to stop Mrs Biswas from moving into the family home. Their conversation lives in my memory with shocking clarity.

'Pa should be careful about ignoring what we

want. I have enough on him to have him extradited.'
George raised his voice, breathing in quick short
bursts, igniting his raging fury. His disapproval
shocked James.

'What are you talking about?'

James went through life with blinkers but loyally
or fearfully supported anything George did.

'How can you not know this? Pa talks when he's
had too many drinks. Surely you remember the night
he told us how he and ma eloped?'

'Can't say that I do, but how is that a legitimate
reason for extradition?' James tapped his fingers on
the table, his agitation heightening with anxiety.

'Pa killed ma's lover, changed his name, and told
the authorities he had no access to his birth certificate
and other papers.'

'Pa is a murderer? Are you sure?'

'Give him half the chance with my protest about
Mrs Biswas moving in, and he will kill me.'

'Don't be stupid, George. Pa won't do such a thing.'

'That's not all. He set the man's home alight,
which killed his mother and...'

'Stop, please stop! I don't want to hear any more
horrid details!'

I knew James to be a tender soul, but he kept silent
whenever George tormented Milly, and sometimes he
joined in on the taunting.

These young men were a chip off the old block or
felt they needed to pretend they were. After hearing

this, I wondered whether they were capable of murder.

That leads me back to Maxwell's mysterious death. I'm not accusing anyone, but this has troubled me for a long time. What if Milly's father was truly capable of such appalling behaviour? This is not something I could tell Norah. She would insist I leave my job, or she might tell baas Albert Sherman. Growing up with my grandmother, I learned unpredictable actions occur when emotions control the reins, especially if fear and anger run wild. You know I said Milly buried her secrets in her inner tomb. Well, my shoulders stooped with the secrets I heard around Milly's family. Poor girl did not know what her brother George claimed to know about their parents. Mrs Romola too was a chamber of secrets!

All this went into my diary.

THE YEAR MILLY TURNED EIGHTEEN, it was a dry season. Part of the sugar plantation, the mid-point, was dryer than the rest of the sugarcane fields. Tinges of green on the outer plants highlighted the golden, browning stalks at the centre. Baas Albert gave no order to clear it, although he was told several times that the section of the field had to be cleared and the soil prepared for a new crop. He drank harder and more often in recent years. Milly's father was spineless in pulling up Albert

Sherman on matters that needed attention on the estate.

I remember the morning as clearly as if it had happened yesterday.

I left Milly at the bus stop. She told her mother she had some shopping to do.

Around 10 am, after Milly's parents went into town, I was cleaning up the yard when I noticed a trickle of smoke rising from the dry centre patch of the plantation.

I investigated, carrying a bush knife. As I cleared my way through the field, I heard a spluttering crackle and popping sound. Coiled flames rose and widened ahead of me. I hurried, frantic with worry that this was the plantation's cremation. I chopped down the dry cane close around me. When I got near the flame, it spiralled and spread like a devil in a wild fire dance. Someone attempted to crawl away from the burning cane.

'Stop, stop, firebug, I have a bush knife!'

'No Edgar! Please, it's me!'

'Who is that? Show yourself, now!'

Master Thomas' head popped up from between the sugarcane stalks. He was whiter than he usually was.

'What are you doing here, Master Thomas?'

'I can't say, but we are leaving now.'

By now I'm sure I was turning pale and must have

been as white as Master Thomas, if that was even possible, when I heard Milly.

'I'm sorry we scared you, Edgar. I told Thomas not to smoke here.'

There was more going on than just Master Thomas smoking. I was complicit in this act and had to get the young lovers to safety and save the plantation.

'Please go home. I saw nothing. Master Thomas, please ask the men to help us put out this blaze. The wind is picking up.'

Milly called out, 'Take care, Thomas.'

'Mill, don't worry, I won't implicate you. Be safe.'

Master Thomas put his palms together and, with begging eyes, he said, 'Thank you, Edgar. I'll get the men.'

He dashed off, stumbling as he hurried.

Milly scrambled home faster than the approaching wind.

The men arrived and doused the angry inferno while baas Albert was out for the day, oblivious and unreachable.

The day haunts me on the possibilities of everything that could have gone wrong for everyone.

Later that evening, baas Albert asked to see Master Thomas and me on his porch.

Master Thomas was wide-eyed and shivering. Perhaps afraid of what I might say.

'Edgar, my man, what happened here today?'

I cleared my throat and had a plan I was toying

with that afternoon on how I would respond if baas Albert questioned me on the situation.

'I saw the smoke as I swept the yard and rushed to check what caused it. When I got to that spot in the plantation, I found Master Thomas putting out the flames that had already started spreading across the field.'

'So, Tommy, here, got there before you?'

Master Thomas appeared ashen and unsteady on his feet. He clutched the porch banister.

'Yes, baas, he bravely prevented the fire from spreading before the men came over to assist.'

'Good man, Tommy, I didn't think you had it in you. What have you got to say?'

'It was a joint effort. Edgar arrived in time for me to get the men over to douse the flames.'

'Good team effort, then. Edgar, you can have the day off tomorrow. Spend the day with Norah and Siya. Go out for the day. You deserve it.'

'Thank you, baas, you are kind. Norah will be pleased.'

Master Thomas looked at me, his eyes red, close to tears.

'Thank you, Edgar,' is all he could say under his father's steady gaze.

When Milly sought me out before I went over to baas Albert's place, I tried to avoid her, but my heart gave in to what my head tried to control.

'Thank you, Edgar, for today. We hope this situation does not bring you trouble.'

'Miss Milly, never say, 'we'—you were not there. I did not see you.'

I touched my heart without looking at her. It was my way of averting my eyes to hide my emotions. I walked away feeling her staring eyes burning the back of my neck. It was far too dangerous to allow Milly to believe I was an ally in her rendezvous with Master Thomas. I knew he had ensnared her heart. She was in deep. I felt it and feared for her safety.

I hoped they would stop their love affair before someone, if not both, got burned by the law and their fathers. Milly would face worse punishment under the country's race prohibition laws. Thomas might get a warning or a fine. His father had power in the area, so he was safe and might mysteriously leave the country.

Milly's secret in the sugar field was my cross to bear.

I would protect Siya in such a situation.

It felt natural to do the same for Milly.

Master Thomas avoided me for a few weeks, awkward perhaps because of the lie we shared. One evening on my walk home, he stopped me at the gate.

'Edgar, wait up, please. I need to talk to you.'

'What is it, Master Thomas?'

'I want to sincerely thank you for protecting me from my father.'

'I don't know if that's such a good thing.'

With lowered head, and his eyes on his boots, he nodded.

'How is Milly? Is she safe from her father's wrath?'

'Now you know you should not be asking me questions about Miss Milly. She seems fine, safe like you.'

'Thank God! I've been worried about her.'

'And you should be. What were you both thinking, being in such a situation?'

'I love Milly with all my heart and would elope with her to Canada, if it were possible.'

'I'll pretend I did not hear that, Master Thomas. Please stop.'

I saw helplessness in his inexperienced eyes.

He held out a note in his trembling hands.

'Please give this to Milly. I have not signed my name on it. You don't have to tell her it's from me. Please, Edgar.'

Sadness infused my being. How could I refuse?

'Leave it under the rock at the outer gate. I'll pick it up on my evening walk. Be sure to conceal it well. Please do not ask me to do this again.'

He whispered his gratitude and left.

That was not the last that Master Thomas sought me out for a favour between the houses. The sugar plantation secrets whispered warnings in the breeze—I was terrified for the lovers and myself.

Milly's and Master Thomas' generation had something to teach the generation that came before them. Especially the men.

Baas Albert had Milly's father chained to him like a docile puppy. No bidding was too much for him. He was a tiger with his wife and daughter, but for baas Albert, he would sell his soul to the devil. When a man compromises his values once, he will do it again.

George's overheard revelation to his brother about his father shaped my impression. Their father had no scruples, and that troubled me.

The first time Mrs Biswas moved in with Milly's father, I knew she would take control. She had a mean streak as one who looked down on the domestic and plantation staff. My work was not up to her expected standard. The floors were not gleaming. The windows were not sparkling. The clothes had to be washed twice. The windowsills had to be wiped twice a day. Dust blowing over from the plantation aggravated her. I knew she could get me fired. Mrs Romola had no say in her living years. This woman commanded everyone with her eyes and strategic comments.

Milly knew I was unhappy and asked me if things were going well with Mrs Biswas. I said it was. I feared she would tell her father to get Mrs Biswas off my back. That would never happen. I saw and heard how he mistreated Milly's mother. Mrs Biswas dressed like the lady of the manor. Painted nails, matching shoes and wide-brimmed hats hid the hardness of her face. She wore well-sewn dresses made at the top end of town. Somehow, she thought race laws did not apply to her.

I noticed her extra care in dressing when she accompanied Milly's father to baas Albert's place on a Sunday evening. This never happened when Milly's mother was alive. I wondered what she did while the two men drank themselves into a stupor.

Norah said nothing on the matter but complained that Mrs Biswas had told baas Sherman that she was not taking good care of his house. The day he spoke to Norah about paying more attention to cleaning the place, an argument broke out between Thomas and his father.

'Pa, please don't listen to the complaints of that woman. This is not her home. You are allowing her too many liberties. Norah is doing a great job cooking, cleaning, and attending to us, as she always has.'

'Now you find your voice, boy, only because you have a soft spot for Norah. I could fire her tomorrow, you know.'

'Nobody knows our needs like Norah. She's irreplaceable. You chose not to remarry after mother died. She has been my mother.'

'I don't want to go into that now. Just leave this to me. It's not your business.'

'Getting rid of Norah is my business. If you do, I'll leave the estate.'

'Hey! You be quiet. You do nothing on the estate except read books and write some rubbish in your precious notebook. I'm watching you and I'm this close to cutting you off from any inheritance.'

Master Thomas walked away, his blood on fire. When his father was in this mood, there was no point in sustaining an argument.

Norah and I were worried about our jobs when Mrs Biswas arrived. Siya told us to leave and move in with her and Zondi.

I could not leave while Milly and Master Thomas needed my protection.

Mrs Biswas was a woman of no morals. I knew she was cooking meals for baas Albert on Sundays, just as Mrs Romola did, but she took it a step further—she 'entertained' him.

Milly's father returned home without her some Sunday evenings. Well after midnight, baas Albert drove her home.

Yes, she was quite the madam, and baas Albert, well, he was the boss.

It rained on Siya's wedding day as if a monsoon hit us. It devastated her that sunny South Africa let her down during the week of her much awaited nuptials. She asked Norah if she was being punished. Norah laughed and said that Milly's mother told her it rained on a wedding day if the bride had eaten from the cooking pot as a young girl. There was some sense in that. Siya always took a quick taste from a hot pot on the stove. When Norah scolded her, she would say, 'Mama, your cooking smells heavenly. How can I resist?' It ended with laughter each time this happened. My two beautiful flowers are graceful, loving and everything to me. I wondered what it would have been like had Siya been a boy. I quickly tossed out that thought when visions of Milly's brother George, and Thomas's brother Henry came to mind. Awful young men, and worse adults. Henry was after his father's wealth and did everything he could to be perceived as the deserving, loyal son. George presented as a hoodlum.

I was happy with my Siya. God chose her for Norah and me. I am grateful for that blessing. The rain made it difficult to socialise outdoors on the wedding day. Continuous rain with a few deceptive stops defined the day.

Siya wanted assurance that the weather was not an ill-fated premonition of her future with Zondi.

'Baba,' she asked, 'do you think the gods are upset?'

'Nonsense, Siya, these are showers of blessings. Just remember that.'

'Oh, baba, I love you. From the time I was a little girl, you've been comforting me.'

'That's what fathers do. I love you very much.'

Norah took a practical, tough-love approach with Siya, hoping it would make her emotionally strong. She scolded me for lavishing too much praise.

'Make her strong enough to stand on her feet, alone, if she is called to do that.'

I smiled and left those comments there. One learns early on that mothers and daughters have a bond that excludes fathers.

The first time Master Thomas Sherman noticed sixteen-year-old Milly—she was hooked. They had been around each other from birth, attending Sunday church and some staff gatherings around Christmas and weddings, but they never socialised. Milly's and Master Thomas' affair was blooming and caught my attention at Siya's wedding. Her eyes were for him alone. Maxwell stood no chance of winning her heart. The flurry of wedding activities pulled me in many directions.

Master Thomas did not attend Siya's wedding but dropped by to offer his congratulations. I noticed Milly was nowhere to be seen after Master Thomas left.

She returned to the wedding reception, drenched to the skin. I took her a towel to dry herself, but she did not care. A content, serene smile lingered on her face, unlike I had ever seen in her. Milly was always neat. A prim little girl and young woman. Now she dropped her guard, and I anticipated trouble.

Today she went through a metamorphosis. She diced with fate in her recklessness.

I said a silent prayer for her safety.

She flitted around all evening trying to avoid Maxwell.

Three months after Siya's wedding, Mr Chiddy arrived at the house as Milly's prospective husband. A wedding was arranged, and baas Albert opened his garden for Milly's big day. A kind gesture indeed.

It was a colourful occasion, but poor Mrs Romola had to cook for the guests. Norah helped her as much as she could. It flummoxed Siya that her dear friend accepted the suitor her parents chose.

'I cannot imagine doing that, and I'm grateful that you and mama accepted my choice of husband.'

'Zondi is a good man. You are blessed.'

Before Mr Chiddy arrived in Milly's life, the secret forbidden relationship between Milly and Master Thomas, continued. Every evening on my walk back to Milly's home, I took to the habit of checking under the rock for a note from Master Thomas. This arrived out of fear that someone's harmful, prying eyes would find it, and she would be in a river of trouble. I had forbidden Master Thomas from ever seeking such favours from me, but I knew his heartbeat for Milly would never end.

How she replied to him once she found the note in her room was beyond me.

She lost her sparkle when she married Mr Chiddy.

I recall the days leading up to Milly's marriage to Mr Chiddy. I saw him visit the family. What an old man, was my initial thought.

An old, sullen man. For all she suffered from her father and brothers, Milly had a cheerful spirit. How would she survive with this unsmiling man? It soon allayed my fears when I perceived his gentle nature.

Not long after that, I saw how well he treated Milly. She asked me to run errands for her and to help her with the house.

'Aye, Miss Milly, I'm getting old now. Are you sure you want me as your house help? I might not be very good at running two houses.'

She laughed and said she did not care how I worked as long as I was around when she needed me. I hoped she did not expect me to continue the favour as a messenger from Master Thomas. She never asked for that favour after she married Chiddy.

God acts in mysterious ways. Mr Chiddy was the husband she needed, not the one she wanted.

It saddened me to see Master Thomas withdraw from interactions on the plantation. I knew depression consumed him. He grieved his loss of Milly. Such was the law of this forsaken land. Love should be free to flourish. It heals. Instead, hatred grew. It deepened and people of colour were restless.

The surging of resistance and talk of a strong unified voice on inequality across the country, gave us courage, but the fight for justice was a long road ahead. I attended secret meetings for updates on the resistance initiatives and Master Thomas was always in attendance—sitting hunched over in the back row. We never spoke about our involvement—it remained our silent commitment. He attended meetings incognito in a trench coat and a wide-brimmed hat. If the police caught him, they would kill him to silence his involvement. At this time of great suffering, the threat of an impimpi selling us out to put food on the table for his family was real. How do you condemn such an act?

Dual allegiances fed hunger and escalated lawlessness.

Siya was outspoken, and I feared for her safety. Somehow Norah convinced her to avoid overreacting as injustice had an end date.

Master Thomas withdrew from all social activities when Mr Chiddy married Milly, but his commitment to the resistance intensified. He never missed a meeting.

One night, we received a tip-off that there was a planned police raid on our meeting. Master Thomas rounded up as many men as he could in his father's van and drove to the plantation. He removed his trench coat and hat, shoved them under his seat and told the men to remain silent. Two minutes into the drive to Sherman's Sugar Estate, police sirens flagged him to stop.

'Remember,' he said to us through clenched teeth, 'keep quiet. I'll do the talking.'

'Good evening officers, what seems to be the problem?'

'Where are you going to with your overloaded van?'

'I am taking these workers to the Sugar Estate. They have an early start tomorrow morning.'

The officers studied Master Thomas' face, then looked at us squashed in the van.

'I suppose you're heading to Sherman's Sugar Estate if you're going in this direction.' The police officer searched our faces, looking for guilt and imprinting our images in his memory.

'That's right, officer. I'm Albert Sherman's son.'

He had to use his family connection to get the men to safety. It worked like a charm.

'Move along, then. Thank your father for the good work he's doing.'

Master Thomas thanked the officer and invited him to visit the plantation.

None of the men, crouching in the van, said a word until we reached the plantation.

They slept in the barn and snuck out in the morning before the sun came up.

I feared a police raid on the estate if there was a leak. Master Thomas had enough literature to mark him as a resistance supporter. He worded the incriminating literature. He was a complex man, different from others in his clan. Passionate, yet vulnerable.

Norah warned me to watch over Master Thomas.

'If you don't protect my boy from harm, I will leave you, Edgar. I'm serious.'

When Norah said, 'I'm serious,' she meant exactly what she said. I had my eyes on Milly and Thomas from the day they were born. I vowed to protect them like my own.

It shocked me to learn that my cousin Solomon was working with the police to snitch on our people. How could someone I called family be a spy? When the resistance movement named him an impimpi, I hung my head in shame. He visited Norah and me often at the plantation, and he was familiar with the lay of the land on baas Albert's property. I worried he would destroy the people closest to me. Was Master Thomas on his hit list? A forgotten memory surfaced of seeing George and Solomon talking in the lane behind the market. They did not know each other, so what could they be chatting about? It felt odd, but I never questioned Solomon about it. I was restless, suspicious of everyone, and needed to be left alone with my thoughts.

When Mrs Biswas's houseboy turned up at the house to assist with domestic chores, a fews months before Mrs Romola passed, it made me uneasy. I watched his every move. This is a terrible thing to do. It brought me a restlessness I could not still. Nobody knew the house boy's name. They referred to him as 'the houseboy.' There was something odd about him. He was silent, avoided eye contact, and left when he finished his chores, telling no one.

Mrs Romola was uncomfortable with his presence, and I overheard her questioning her husband about why he brought the boy to work at the house.

'We need another person to help us with chores, especially in the garden. Edgar has a lot to do, and as he gets older, we need to train the houseboy to take over from him.'

'Edgar is good and coping well. I don't like the houseboy, Arnold.'

He ignored Mrs Romola's plea. With the news of Solomon's impimpi activities, I contemplated whether the houseboy worked with Solomon. That would make him a spy in our home! This torrid time in South Africa baffled us. If trust breaks down, life is a living hell. I transgressed in my expected allegiance to Mr Arnold. I reserved it for Mrs Romola and Milly. When Mrs Romola befriended a Chinese lady who was a stallholder at the market, it infuriated Mr Arnold, who then told her she could not go to the markets with me. Their friendship started as a shared interest in embroidery. Maisie Tran, the stallholder, allowed Mrs Romola to sell her embroidery tray cloths and other pieces at her stall for a small fee. After Mr Arnold prohibited their friendship, I secretly took the embroidery work Mrs Romola made to Maisie Tran and collected Mrs Romola's earnings from the sale. She insisted I take a portion of her earnings, but I refused. I knew why Mr Arnold reacted this way to her friendship with Maisie Tran. Mrs Biswas was not from the indentured immigrant class. Her family came to South Africa as business immigrants. It gave them some status, I suppose, and Mr Arnold protected Mrs Biswas and her clan from losing business through immigrants like Maisie Tran. Mrs Romola was a good woman who deserved a better life. Our children struck up a friendship because she allowed it. It brought her joy to see our daughters wonderful growing-up years.

Mrs Romola and Milly were family to us. It compelled me to protect them within my capacity.

Master Thomas sensed my concern regarding Soloman, and waited at the gate of his father's property for my return from work.

'Good evening, Edgar. May I have a quick word, please?'

I kept my eyes on the ground, afraid of what he was about to say.

'What is it, Master Thomas?'

'I don't want you to worry about what Solomon has done. He won't come back to the plantation now. The police will have him in a safe place because the word is out about his activities.'

'Thank you, Master Thomas.'

That was all he said.

I could not tell him I was afraid they might kill him. Or that my cousin Solomon's wife, four children, and a fifth child on the way needed my support. I had to work out how to help his family without creating the suspicion that I was supporting his activities. Master Thomas pressed my shoulder and walked back to the house.

Challenges arrived uninvited, and if I was a loyal man of God, I had to help the vulnerable. A moral conscience becomes a formidable enemy if you ignore its cries.

Political troubles brewed on the outside, and domestic matters churned with equal force inside. The conditions in the country fostered an aggressive male attitude, leaving our women voiceless. I had to do the right thing for Norah, Siya, and Milly, but I had to remain voiceless on some of Milly's issues.

I questioned myself if Siya was Milly, would I want the bearer of her painful truth to expose her? Would I expect that person to tell me my daughter's secrets?

The answer was always an emphatic no.

A loyal friend, protector, whatever label a person like me attracts should remain true to the person he or she protects. Milly's only guilt, if one could call it that, was loving across the colour bar. The same applied to Master Thomas.

Both were not sinners for loving each other. Mr Chiddy's innocent ignorance disturbed me. That was on Milly's head, and I sincerely pitied her having that on her conscience.

I am grateful that I worked on Sherman's Sugar Estate because the atrocities at other plantations seeped out that young men faced torture, some left for dead, others struggled with malnutrition and endured a host of unhygienic abhorrent conditions. Inhumane plantation owners had blood on their hands but continued to flog their men, to toil the fields for their financial gain. The mines never attracted me. I could not be away from Norah and Siya for long spells. My earnings were not much, but my family was with me. That makes me grateful to baas Albert. He used his power over his workers with threats of terminating their service if they displeased him, but he provided reasonable accommodation and meals during the cutting and planting season. Loyalty was everything to him, and Milly's father did that well. It earned him many favours. He was a token white man in his suit with a family car gifted to him by baas Albert. He never used it for family outings. I drove Milly and her mother wherever they wanted to go. George and his father drove the family Chevrolet bakkie. Many young women rode around with George, but Milly did not have that privilege as his family.

THE DAY MASTER THOMAS DIED, he took a part of Norah with him. She lost her confidence and sense of joy. She could not understand his death and I could not tell her what I knew. I gave my trust to Milly and Thomas, and I vowed I would take it to my grave. My beautiful, loving Norah never smiled again.

The day Master Thomas died; I lost my Norah.

A lot remained unspoken in my family on Master Thomas' death. I was grateful that Siya did not ask questions. She was preoccupied with her mother's descent into depression. I often found Norah sitting out in the backyard, staring into space. She was spectral thin, forgetting to eat, or refusing to eat. She sipped on tea and nibbled bits of toast, nothing more. Her heart loved with the intensity of a mother who had lost her child in an awful tragedy. I understood and stayed close by her side until the end. Master Thomas, the dear boy, left her financially secure. They say the good die young. Regardless of how he passed, Master Thomas was a good man. Plantation owners enchained us, but the human heart could never remain eternally subjugated behind racial lines. Master Thomas, Milly, and Norah proved this. I missed Master Thomas' presence, but had to hold my sorrow within. I had to be strong for Norah and Milly. Master Thomas was the love of their lives. I understood we forget the lifetime of a man in death, but his last act of love remains forever.

At the tender age of ten, Master Thomas turned to me with questions that troubled him. His father would never entertain questions not related to the sugar plantation.

'Why are people treated differently? God created all people, right? That's what we learn in church, but why are some so poor and others treated like they don't matter?'

'Don't worry, that young head of yours, Master Thomas. Go along and get on with what is important to you. Enjoy your day. The sun is shining, it is a beautiful day.'

'What troubles me is important to me. Why am I expected to call you Edgar when you are much older than me, and perhaps pa too, yet you call me Master Thomas? From today, I will call you Mr Edgar.'

'Now, now, Master Thomas, you know that will get you into trouble.'

'With whom, Mr Edgar?'

His cheeky grin warmed my heart. He was a child with a deep soul, someone who could make a vast difference in this country someday, but I had such fear that he would invite trouble with such talk. Trouble he could not extricate himself from. I had to tell him his father was a good man.

'Look, Master Thomas, baas Albert has a good heart. My family and I live comfortably here on the sugar estate. We have a roof over our heads, food, and water, and your father ensures Siya has books to read, and I get to read his daily newspaper after he has read it. He treats us like family, and I respect that.'

'Then you should live in the house with us, not at the back of the building. I would love it if you lived in the house.'

This tender-hearted lad was innocent to the ways of the world. What would happen to him when he wizened up to the atrocities on other plantations? My prayer was for him to have his father's adoration, for baas Albert to accept that his children were different. Master Thomas was every bit like his mother. Her dreamy, compassionate nature isolated her from the other plantation owners' wives. Parties did not interest her, neither did afternoon tea with the ladies. Young Master Thomas knew nothing of his mother's ways, but Norah ensured she nurtured his soft-hearted side. Norah said Mrs Sherman treated her like an equal, always checking if she was coping with the work she had to do, offering to take some things off her, reminding her she had a child to care for too. The large parties baas Albert insisted on hosting made her sad. Too much judgement, competition, and beady eyes on the hostess' dress sense. Master Thomas' mother was a simple woman, the salt of the earth. The good die young is the truth I know.

Why is it that only when there is loss and grief that we feel the value of lost time like a soul gnawing ache? My mother, too, was the salt of the earth. The only parent I knew. My father died in our house fire when he saved my mother and me, barely two months old. A candle blew off the table in the wind and a dry winter season made our little hut a tinder box. My mother told me when I was much older that he pushed us out before crackling, raging flames engulfed him. The remote location we lived in had no access to fire services and water had to be drawn from a well shared by a cluster of huts. My mother struggled to raise me on her own. In the little patch of garden, we called our own; she grew potatoes and onions and took it to the market. After a few years, she set up a stall on the roadside, close to the market, to make a few extra coins. The large market management took a big cut as their commission, which forced her to go on her own for our survival.

One day I returned from school and heated the water waiting for her to come home. I was twelve years old. July was a harsh month with drought making vegetable growth difficult. When she did not return home that evening, I walked to the spot where she had her makeshift store. It was beside a busy free-way. She was not there. I saw people walk by and called out to them, 'Have you seen my mama? She sells potatoes and onions here.' Some onlookers stared at me, and told me to go home, that it was dangerous to be loitering on this busy stretch of road. One lady stopped and helped me. She lit her candle and asked if the basket tossed on the grassy strip belonged to my mother. It lay there flattened—there was no sign of my mother. 'Go home, *Umntwana*. I will tell the police your mother is missing.' I grabbed her hand. 'Please let me come with you to the police station. I can describe my mother to them.' She nodded, and I caught the sadness in her eyes as the waning candle glimmered across her face.

'Where could my mama be?' I was close to tears and afraid.

'*Angaas*, my dear,' she whispered, and we walked the rest of the way to the police station in silence that heightened the sound of the icy wind ripping through the trees. The police told me to go home and that my mother would return soon. They took no details. I was orphaned without knowing what happened to my mother. My maternal grandmother, Eunice, moved into our home. I asked my uncle Silas, my mother's brother, to help me find out what happened to my mother. My grandmother said, 'Don't waste your time, Edgar. Silas is a drunk. Let's pray your mother is at rest wherever she is.' When I asked her if she thought my mama was dead, she shrugged her shoulders and said, 'It's better to think she is. That will bring you some peace, my boy.' I could not understand her logic. How could she accept her daughter was dead and expect me to do the same? Now, at this mature age, I understand the wisdom of her words. Something awful happened that day alongside the freeway. I played out the imagined scenes repeatedly in my mind. I finally accepted that a truck that sped on that stretch of road had struck her. The driver never reported the incident... I accepted that and had to move on with my life. My hardworking mama left me too soon.

I had no answers about why I was orphaned at twelve, but as the silent worker in a turbulent household, you see and know much. You form your private allegiances and hold their secrets close to your heart. You go unnoticed, but you have the power to unremittingly support or destroy.

With the diary locked and labelled, *For Milly*, I placed it in a file box with my other private papers and left it with the lawyer who wrote up my will. Burying the box deep in the middle of the sugar plantation in the space that separated Milly's childhood home from baas Albert Sherman and his boy, Thomas, came to mind. But, unsavoury hands might sully what happiness she might have found in later years.

I did not expect the horror that would follow Milly years later.

———

SECRETS DIMINISH WITH DEATH.

PART FOUR

MILLY

The blood of two men stained my life.

I found my mother's private record of her life at the bottom of her wooden chest, soon after she passed. She pinned the key to her petticoat. How she avoided detection from my father is beyond me. She wrote her secret heart on the unused pages of my school exercise books. A clever ploy to hide her truth from the man she feared more than she could ever love.

I opened my mother's secret chest again when Chiddy fell ill. I felt I had to let him into our family's secrets before he was called to his last rest. He turned his back on his family when their tongues wagged around Sugar's birth. He was a good, kind man. This is why my mother chose him for me. Her hardship made a good judge of character.

I held the secret knowledge of my mother's journals to myself.

After reading some of her entries, I locked the chest and tried to erase the memory of her words.

The first exercise book I opened had an inscription on the inside cover which read: *Me*. What lay within stole my breath.

I was sixteen years old and two months carrying a child when I left my mother's house for my sea voyage on the Umlazi. I left with the man who was not my heart's choice. He forced his attention on me. I ignored him until I found myself in a situation I could not rectify. My love, my only love, was dead. Murdered. I could not be an unwed mother bringing disgrace to my family.

I left with Dahak, a tough and cruel man.

He was, I thought, my passport to freedom, a new beginning.

We arrived in South Africa after almost two months on rough seas that tossed us about like tattered foam chips. I was sick for most of the journey. Dahak paid no attention to me. The ship manager separated us onboard, or perhaps he stayed away from me by choice.

Dahak registered our marriage upon arrival, claiming family members destroyed our identity documents. He changed his name to Arnold and mine to Romola. As Arnold, he was determined to make a success of his life in what he called The Promised Land. Albert Sherman took a liking to him and we moved into Sherman's Sugar Estate. From that day, Mr Sherman was Arnold's idol. If he could put a garland around his neck and prostrate at his feet, he would have enjoyed that. At first, we had a modest home—a barn converted into living quarters. The toilet was a long walk from the barn. We slept on bundled old calico sugar bags. A small coal stove and an outside tap were all we had.

It was here, in my first year of marriage, where James was born.

The baby looked everything like me. He was a mild-mannered child, much to

Arnold's annoyance. When George was born eighteen months later, Arnold celebrated that he was bigger and bold. George was his favourite—even a stranger could see that. George bullied poor James. I protected him as much as possible, but he soon embraced George's attitude when Milly arrived. Both bullied and teased her with a harshness that saddened me.

Milly brought me joy. Arnold droned on about girls being a nuisance—they cost too much to maintain was his endless moan.

Albert Sherman looked after Arnold, which made our lives bearable. We had food and better living quarters after Milly was born. So many people who arrived at the same time we did, had little to nothing.

I SHUT the book when rising palpitations made me weak.

This was the first time I had any inkling of my mother's life before my birth. The pattern was unfolding. My father brought my mother with him to take care of him. He saw her kind and giving nature and exploited that. Did he love her? That was never apparent to me.

My darling brother James passed before Candy got

married. A bout of pneumonia claimed him. He never married, remaining a solitary figure. He adored Sugar and Zola and lavished them with gifts as a loving uncle. I wondered whether he knew the nature of his birth. New wounds surfaced through my mother's angst.

I had to return to the locked chest.

Would I be able to help Candy once our family's transgressions were open for scrutiny?

I forced myself to reopen the exercise book on my mother's life.

Arnold ensured there was no evidence or history of our lives in the motherland. It made us self-proclaimed orphans. I had the shame of an illegitimate child, but he had a darker past. Mine was a cultural shame—his was punishable by law.

I stashed the exercise book at the bottom of the chest and picked up another book that bore my name in my mother's handwriting. I tucked it into the wooden chest, under a pile of my mother's scarves, afraid and not ready to face my demons.

It took a week before I dared to reopen the chest. Ma labeled a third exercise book, *Mabel Biswas*—the third person in my mother's marriage.

The first time I had the misfortune of seeing the widow Mabel Biswas, I sensed something between her and Arnold. Every Sunday at church, he went over to greet her, and she spoke to him with downcast eyes and fleeting looks in my direction. I knew the late nights and early mornings when he returned home after being with her. He was never hungry when he got home. She fed him well. Whenever he had a carousal with Albert Sherman, he came home ravenous, rattling the pots, demanding food, and disturbing the children. When he asked me to bake an extra Christmas cake for a struggling family, I knew he lied. He took the cake to Mrs Biswas. I accepted the situation because there was nothing I could do about it. We needed a home and food for our children. When Mrs Saldana asked her husband to leave his concubine, she was homeless until a plantation owner took her on as a housemaid. Poor woman, her life changed because she spoke up. I did not love Arnold; I cared about his well-being, but each time he

returned from Mabel Biswas, I felt
worthless, wretched, unwanted, and ugly.
She knew I knew and did not end the
situation. I noticed her two pregnancies
that she tried to conceal. Then, in the latter
stages, she stayed away from the
public eye.

Johnny and Lizzy are Arnold's
children.

I lived this life from the day James
was born.

We should never give a man the power to steal our self-confidence—we who serve them in sickness and health. Oh, how I wish I knew this before my mother died. She was stoic, yet her pain on these pages was palpable. I read these private thoughts and know that Chiddy was a good man. My mother gave a nod of approval for my union with him, believing he would treat me right. How could she have ever trusted a man after what my father put her through? I contemplated how much I would share of my findings with Sugar, Zola, and Candy.

My mother deserved the preservation of her dignity in death. I would expect my daughters to honour that. I fear I do not deserve such dignity. People say *like mother like daughter*, but my daughters had no secrets. With that knowledge, I felt safe. I prayed for that after delving into my mother's past. She led a lonely life, isolating herself to ensure she did not confide in anyone about her domestic trauma. I'm glad such a time has passed, that women can speak their truths and hold their own in the world. Equality is a righteous way to happiness and a peaceful life. Deception festers when gender equality is denied.

Lies are a false shield to superficial displays of harmony.

My mother's era has passed, but I know that there are women who live under a similar veil, accepting that they are powerless to change their status quo. I pondered over the sort of life my maternal grand-mother might have had. I drew a blank there. My mother sealed that portal to her childhood. I cannot imagine my daughters doing that to me. I was on the brink of their wrath with Jadon's birth. It left me sleepless.

I did not have to explain my hours in the basement reading my mother's heart to Chiddy. He did not ask, and his poor knees kept him confined to those parts of the house that did not have stairs. I toyed with revealing what he might already know about my life. I never knew then that I would have to unveil all I knew to my granddaughter.

Chiddy never got to hear the truth from me. He died before Jadon was born. He was unwell for a few months leading up to our great-grandson's birth.

Births and deaths seem to work in sync in some families. I knew of countless such situations. Give and take, the circle of life. We had a small funeral on Sherman's Estate with the workers in attendance. His family never responded to my message that he had passed peacefully. After Chiddy passed I left my mother's journals locked in secrecy. Now, Candy wanted answers on our ancestry.

Chiddy knew the truth, but never asked for clarification. How could he not know, living with my superficial interactions?

When Candy gave me an ultimatum to unveil our family history, I was terrified that she would stop loving me. My Candy girl. I owed her the truth if I hoped to have a small part in little Jadon's life. The decision to tell the full truth rested in my corner.

She wanted baby Jadon to have his father in his life. She loved Terence, and now their family faced separation because his grandmother filled his head with questions. The worst is the untruth that he might not be Jadon's father.

It had to be told soon.

I had to find peace before I took my eternal rest.

The archives of my mind yielded memories that melded my angst and joy. How could both exist in one life? I am a good person. I know that. My love for Thomas was the only thing I did that made me a bad person in the eyes of a twisted legal system. He came to me when he felt the call of my heartbeat whenever he was near me. Forbidden, yet the sweetest fruit in my life.

The day Siya got married, I knew Thomas was the only love for me. He had watched me but never told me how he felt. One day, before we accepted our mutual throbbing hearts, I walked over to Albert Sherman's property with my father. He was a little unwell, and my mother asked me to help him carry over the food she prepared for Mr Sherman's Sunday dinner.

I spotted Thomas riding the family white horse. My heart raced.

'Oh, how I wish we had such a horse.'

My father shook his head. 'Get rid of that silly idea. We could never afford it. Perhaps Mr Sherman will let you have a closer look at his horse.'

He said nothing to Thomas' father. When Mr Sherman asked me how I was, I gushed about how beautiful the white horse was.

'Take a walk to the stable, Milly. Thomas will bring Gracie in from his ride. Tell him I sent you to have a look at her.'

'Thank you so much, Mr Sherman.'

'I think Milly should be home before it's too late.'

'Nonsense, let her have a quick look, then she can walk back home.'

I dashed out before my father protested again. He could lie saying I had allergies or create some such fabrication.

Thomas was brushing Gracie down when I peeked

in at the stable door. He did not know I was watching him.

'Excuse me, Master Thomas. Your father said I could come over to see Gracie. Is now a good time?'

'Come in,' he smiled, 'it is a good time, but please don't call me master. You can help me brush Gracie down.'

'Thank you!'

He gave me the hand brush and pulled out a stool from the shelf to allow me to reach Gracie's neck.

'She's so elegant,' I whispered.

Thomas smiled, observing my movements.

'Do you love animals, Milly?'

His voice was velvety soft, and kindness oozed from his bright blue eyes.

'I do, but we only have chickens that go into the pot. I love dogs.'

'You should have a pet then. I'll talk to my father.'

'No, please don't. It might anger my father.'

'Why?'

'It's better we don't ask, please.'

Thomas nodded and was quiet for the rest of the time I spent in the stable with him and Gracie. The awkward sense of his presence made me thank him and head home. He smiled and nodded, saying in a soft voice, 'Come over whenever you want to see Gracie.'

It was not up to me if I could ever do that again.

Siya's sixteenth birthday lit the fire inside me

when I saw Thomas appear at the door looking for my brother, George.

Our first meeting alone was when I saw him standing close to the bus stop where I disembarked after school. My stop was the last. Nobody else was on board the bus. As soon as the bus was out of sight, Thomas walked up to me.

'Can we talk, Milly? I'll walk home with you.'

'I will be in a load of trouble if my father sees me walking home with you. Edgar is not picking me up today, so let's talk behind the bus shelter. The next bus arrives in an hour hour.'

'I don't understand why you'll be in trouble. We will just be walking home.'

I was the first to open my heart.

'Thomas, what is prohibited for both of us, could put me in a lot of trouble, not only with my father but the law, too.'

His melting look made me weak in the knees.

'I can't stop thinking about you, Milly. I love you.'

'No! You cannot say that! What are we going to do? This you and I cannot be. I can't...'

'We can be super careful when we meet. Please Milly, say yes.'

He held me close, kissed me and we clung to each other. I had never felt such love before, and clung to him afraid this was a fleeting moment.

'We must find another way. Meeting like this will work for a while.'

'I know, we can change the location, each time, to avoid being found out.'

We sealed our love with a stolen kiss that afternoon behind the bus shelter.

There were days when we met at the beach, but each time, all we had was ten stolen minutes. I could never leave the house at night without my brothers knowing, and there was an unspoken police curfew for indigenous people, which meant they were on the prowl. We were playing with fire, but the addiction to being with each other made taking risks exciting. Then Thomas had an idea.

'We could meet on the plantation field. The men stop work at 2:30 pm to attend to the gardens and animals. The deserted plantation will offer us cover from being seen together.'

I was dubious with both our houses being across the plantation, at opposite ends.

'We can't meet there often. You know that.'

'I promise I won't put you in any danger, Milly, please say yes.'

I agreed with a level of trepidation, but the absolute freedom we felt in the field had us taking too many risks.

At Siya's wedding, I used the celebratory distraction to meet Thomas outside the reception venue. Rain was the blessing that allowed us to go unnoticed.

Thomas was not himself that day.

'Is something wrong, Thomas?'

He looked at me with his big blue eyes and shook his head.

'You're lying. Please tell me what's bothering you.'

'Are you faithful to me?'

'How can you ask me such a question?'

'I've noticed Siya's friend hanging around you.'

'Maxwell?'

He nodded and looked away.

'He knows I'm not interested in him, and all I will be is a friend.'

Thomas was broody, so different to the boy who first met me behind the bus shelter.

'I hope you trust me on that.'

He nodded, pulled me close, and dragged me into the rain.

Before he left, he whispered in my ear, 'I am saving all I can to elope with you to Canada, where our love can be free.'

I hung onto that hope with every breath I had.

Months rolled on until Edgar discovered our secret in the sugarcane field. I was afraid he would tell my father or Thomas' father. He kept my secret but warned me to forget Thomas. How could I? It was the first time I felt loved, free from judgement, just loved for being me. Thomas got around Edgar and secret anonymous notes arrived in my room.

Thomas had a way with words. He wrote beautiful love poems and copied lines from his favourite poets.

Come away with me my love!
  To build a bed of roses
  Not for a season, but a lifetime

Come away with me my love!
  Together we will survive
  Life's storms—our petals strong

Come away with me my love!
  To live and love as freely as the lark.
  Singing our hearts' song

Come away with me my love!
  Where the sun shines eternal
  And the moon no shadow casts

Come away with me my love!
  Across the vast blue ocean where love thrives

I rewrote Thomas' poems to keep them safe in my handwriting. I held onto his lines for a few days, then cut them into miniscule pieces and set them out in the wind.

Thomas was hopeful, and I clung to his optimism as racial divisiveness ulcerated the beautiful land we both called home. His support of the underground movement against inequality earned him the title of 'White Spook.' He prepared slogans and wrote letters to overseas leaders of many countries, spreading awareness on the growing struggles of people of colour in South Africa. We spoke about the injustice perpetrated by the government. He bemoaned his father's and brother's lack of involvement in counteracting injustice.

My mother's silent knowledge about my secret love affair guided her choice of Chiddy as a suitable husband for me. My father gave her no credit for intuition and intelligence, but secrecy was her superpower. She rubbed my growing belly; hidden under baggy clothes I could not conceal from her knowing eyes.

'Some day you will thank me for this.' She whispered into my hair.

How? The father of my unborn child did not know I was carrying his child. Our only child.

I am grateful to my mother for protecting me from my father's rage...but my heart was unchangeable.

Chiddy accepted me with no questions. In the intimacy of our married life, my swelling belly was obvious. He never forced himself on me, waiting until Sugar was born before he touched me. That made him a saint. My inner critic did a fine job of making me feel worthless. All I got from Chiddy was silent respect. I needed that while I grieved for my lost love. My husband and mother were identical in their silent acceptance of what they bore with stoicism. My daughters, Sugar and Zola, received unwavering love in our home. I gave Chiddy unflinching respect, but could not love him. My heart belonged to Thomas.

My father was a raging bull when alcohol inflamed his temper. I know he slapped and shoved my mother around when something angered him. She covered her head with a scarf, which she drew across her face to conceal her swollen jaw. I saw the blue marks on her uncovered arms. My heart ached when I watched her swabbing her arms with warm salted water. My brothers knew she was being abused. They turned up the music in their rooms and locked me in my room.

Edgar knew my mother's troubles. Whenever she wore a headscarf, I heard him say, 'Mrs Romola, you rest today. I'll do the cooking. I'll bring tea and a sandwich in an hour.'

She did as he said because she knew he would let her know if my father's van came down the dusty road behind our house.

Today, reading through my mother's life, I am filled with a deep sadness for what I did not do to help her. Things I could not undo.

The day I married Chiddy, Edgar stopped being the bearer of Thomas' love notes.

The letter I received from Thomas came in the mail before Sugar was born. Edgar collected and distributed the mail from our letterbox. He handed me the envelope with downcast eyes. I whispered my thanks, locked myself in the bathroom, and ripped the envelope open.

DEAREST MILL,

I hope you are well, and happy with the man you have married. Norah told me you are having a baby.

My calculation makes me believe you are carrying our child.

Mill, please tell me I am right. I will not disturb the life that was chosen for you. But please, I beg you, confirm what I already know. It will be impossible to meet, I understand. Come to church on Sunday and give me a sign, a nod, or wear that pretty pink bow in your hair that you wore at our first meeting behind the bus shelter. Please, Mill, that is all I ask. You have not been to church since your wedding day. Burn this letter after reading it.

THE UNSIGNED LETTER CARRIED THOMAS' anguished voice.

I did not go to church that Sunday and never saw Thomas again.

The week Sugar was born, whispers floated around the plantation and into town that Sugar looked like a white baby. The whispers never ceased.

The year Sugar turned sixteen, Thomas died. He was found hanging in the stable where he let me brush and stroke his father's prize mare, Gracie.

I mourned his death in the silence I observed in my mother. Raising Sugar was all I lived for. She kept Thomas alive for me.

Three months after Thomas passed, Edgar drove me to the beach where Thomas and I spent fleeting sweet stolen hours.

'What's this about, Edgar? Has something happened?'

He looked away, and I felt fear gnaw at my insides.

In a whisper he said, 'There is something from Master Thomas for you. He asked that I drive you here and hand over this file box to you.'

'What's inside? I'm so afraid to look.'

'I don't know, but I can say with certainty it will be full of love. You look through the box and take a walk on the beach. I'll be back in an hour. Is that ok, Miss Milly?'

'No, Edgar, please stay with me as I do this.'

I opened the file box with a pounding heart. Tears veiled my eyes. Tears I had to conceal upon news of his untimely passing.

The letter from Thomas said it all.

My dearest Mill,

I am deeply sorry that I cannot be here beside you to tell you my plans for our daughter. It is unbearable that I am the father of our beautiful child, a young woman now, who will never know me, not in this life. I dreamed of our elopement and life together. It was not to be.

Please allow me to be the unnamed father to Sugar through all that I am leaving for her and you. The documents contained herein are the bank accounts, one in your name, the other in Sugar's, which you will manage for her until you see fit to hand it over to her. How you will ever explain this to her is up to you, but I ask that she never be told that I was her father. It will bring her untold sorrow which I want to protect her from ever feeling. I hope you understand. My share of Sherman's Estate is bequeathed to Sugar. I hope my brother honours this. I lodged everything with my attorney, Philip Jacobson, in Johannesburg. The house I purchased in Umhlanga is out on rent—the title deeds are in your name.

If someone ever displaces you from the sugar plantation property, please move into the Umhlanga home. Your husband, Chiddy, is welcome to live there with you.

You have my heart forevermore. If the title deeds are in your name, no race laws, I believe, can prohibit you from living there. If I'm wrong sell the house and settle wherever you wish.

I'm sorry—there was no other way. How do I go on

living knowing you and Sugar are walking distance away from me? I am grateful for the good father Chiddy is for our girl.

I take your love with me. It kept me whole in the living years. Be happy for me, my love. Do not grieve, I chose this to free myself from this constant pain of not being with you and our daughter.

We shall meet again when you arrive where racial laws do not exist to separate us.

His second unsigned letter left me in a daze. My head spun, and I was nauseous. I held onto my seat, swaying with uncontrollable sobs. Edgar jumped out of the vehicle and walked over to the passenger seat.

'Are you unwell, Miss Milly? Should I drive you to the family doctor?'

'No, please drive me home, but first, I want to walk on the beach.'

'Are you sure you want to walk alone, Miss Milly?'

'Yes please, Edgar. This shocking yet loving news has ripped my heart open. Thomas, my darling Thomas, died for me.'

Edgar was silent. He held my hand—something he had never done before.

'He's left everything to Sugar and me.'

I heard Edgar's heavy, low voice. 'Master Thomas was a special person. A good man.'

I had to process this before I returned to the plantation.

Edgar waited in the van while I took a slow,

pensive walk on the beach. I sat on the rock where Thomas and I clung to each other in our precious secret moments. His presence pulsated through me when I closed my eyes. I felt his arm across my shoulder, just as he would do when we sat here, on the rock, watching the waves lap up on the shore. I shouted out my gratitude for the love shared, for Sugar and the legacy he left her, and felt the wind ripple across my face like loving fingers. Walking with slow, deliberate steps to make the moment last, I promised myself I would never return to this rock. This was not my last farewell to my love. This moment, like the few we spent together, would sustain me.

Edgar drove me home in his usual silence. He never spoke of Thomas again.

I slept in the lounge for three nights. Chiddy said nothing. One evening he nudged my arm, and I opened my eyes. He offered me a cup of tea, nodded, and walked away as I touched his hand and thanked him.

I contemplated the sadness Chiddy was enduring on my account and went back to our bedroom the next night.

THE MEMORIES of Thomas never left me. He had deep-seated father issues. He felt unloved and worthless. We talked about what he perceived as his failings. He was not cut out for plantation work, and his father did not understand that. He yearned to go to England to live with his maternal grandparents.

Albert Sherman blocked his communication with them. He was a proud man and vowed that he would raise his sons without their help. Thomas faced sharp criticisms whenever he showed his artistic side.

'At least you have your mum, Mill. I am grateful for Norah, who has been a protector and provider of emotional support. I embrace her as my forever mother.'

'That's beautiful. Norah is a special person. You and Siya are fortunate to have been raised by her.'

'Do you share a close bond with your mother?'

I paused, not wanting to create a poor impression of my struggling mother.

'She is the best mother a child could ask for. Sadly, she cannot stand up to my father's bullying.'

'That's sad. I wish I could help you here.

'Thank you, but please don't go there. It will unleash my father's anger. Nobody from outside our family knows his horrible side. He is a Jekyll and Hyde. If you intervene, he will know his children are spreading his stink around the plantation. That will be the end of me. He dotes on the boys. Please let it be.'

'I will do nothing to harm you. Please believe me.'

'I do.'

Sharing our family secrets lightened the weight we carried.

Thomas loved cricket and joined a local club. I could not attend his matches on a Sunday afternoon, but George could support Thomas. He had to sit on the grass to the side of the stand. Racial laws prohibited sitting with white folk at sporting events and other public places. I questioned my relationship with Thomas, but I could not undo what my heart had unlocked. He was oblivious to colour and treated everyone with compassion and respect.

I returned to my mother's journal entries. I was on a timeframe from Candy and Sugar, to provide the details they needed. If Candy could not save her marriage, it would be my fault to bear now and in the afterlife.

An entry my mother had written during her illness caught my attention.

Brutality follows me in this doomed life. I pray that in my next life, I'm free from this curse. Why has violence defined my life's circumstances? Another force influenced George, and I know he killed Maxwell. I heard him leave late one night and peered out my room door. He dressed in black clothes. I heard him rummage in the garage before a car picked him up outside the house. Soon after that night, we heard Maxwell was missing and later found murdered. Somebody else was involved, but I will go to my grave not knowing the truth. George is my son. What is a mother to do?

A COLD SWEAT erupted on my nose bridge up to my hairline. My hands shook like one with delirium tremors. I suspected George was involved in Maxwell's disappearance. My mother confirmed he had an accomplice. I lay on the couch, troubled by my family's dark and terrible deeds. My father made my mother an accomplice to his crime by eloping with her to escape the justice system. How would my daughters react to this heinous information?

Many more entries were beckoning my acknowledgment. My heart and mind needed a break.

The clock was ticking for Candy's request.

I gathered my thoughts and decided it would be better to write a letter to Sugar and Candy once I had gone through all my mother's journal entries. Part of me wanted to burn the unread pages. Maxwell's death bothers me. George held the key to the details, but his advancing dementia made that impossible.

I imagined the conversation we would have if his

memory served him well.

'I know you were involved in Maxwell's disappearance. Ma told me someone else was involved. Who was it?'

I believed he would be angry and resistant to my question.

'Is ma speaking to you from the grave?'

There would be that characteristic cold sneer in his voice of the younger George I grew up with. Now he was a shadow of his former self, and I felt pity for him.

'Please tell me, was pa involved?'

'I refuse to answer that question. It's closer to you than you know.'

'I don't believe that.'

'I knew you would say that. Good night, Milly.'

He would hang up on me like he had done countless times before when I offered to take care of him.

George was a strong-willed man. He could pass in a matter of days or drag on. Regardless of what he had done, he was family, and I wanted to help.

George was unchangeable. This apple did not fall too far...

I left my imagination on that note.

When life throws you a curve that threatens relationships, you cannot allow those closest to you, from a time past, to return to fill your head and heart with memories you want to forget, yet wish you could conjure into the present again.

My mother and Edgar dwelled within me through

my trials.

EDGAR DIED AFTER CHIDDY, at the grand age of a hundred and six, according to his calculation. There was no record of his birth.

He comforted me in his usual silent way when Chiddy passed, but accepted that I hid my pain when Thomas departed this life. The Umgeni church was packed on Edgar's funeral day. People spilled out onto the courtyard, standing in scorching Natal heat, sweat and tears intermingling.

I sat in the first row, close to Edgar's coffin. Sugar sat to my left and Zola to my right. My mind wandered to Thomas, my only love, Chiddy, the faithful, giving husband, and Edgar, the loyal, honest keeper of my truth. All three men were pillars in my struggles. Thomas, the briefest candle of them all, took my heart with him. Here, Edgar lay, ten years after Norah crept away in her sleep. Pastor Madlala asked me to conduct Edgar's eulogy, but I was fragile and weary. I wrote the eulogy, and Sugar delivered it on the day.

Pastor Madlala officiated a sermon and tribute to Edgar that reduced every heart to rivulets of loving tears. He referred to Edgar as his father, brother, and son of the church. God's messenger of kindness and compassion. We were privileged to have him walk among us.

For most of my life, I avoided political discussions. Today I unleashed my silence in Edgar's eulogy. Sugar stood tall and strong as always—she looked me in the eye and spoke as I would.

I deliver our dearest Edgar's eulogy today, on behalf of my mother, for a man who stood by our family, putting his needs aside, throughout the years we were blessed to have him under our roof. These are my mother's words:

Edgar was my silent advisor and compassionate listener. He was my rock and pillar but never stone hearted in comforting me during my tough days. A devoted husband to the late Norah, and ever-loving father of Siya, Edgar looked at everyone on Sherman's Sugar Estate with equal respect. From Mr Sherman to my family and the plantation workers, permanent or itinerant, he gave the same kindness and respect.

This country has much to learn from Edgar Wiseman Dlamini, aptly named, living his values up to his last breath. His gentle manner touched us all, especially my mother, Romola, who called him Goodman Edgar when referring to him. To Siya, I say, your Baba will never leave us—he will continue to watch over us and guide our actions. In you, he gave me a sister for which I am forever grateful.

May our beloved Edgar Wiseman Dlamini rest cradled in eternal peace until we meet again.

God save us all.

Hamba Kahle, my dear brother, Edgar.

It felt surreal to farewell Edgar through my words

in Sugar's voice. He protected her with courage and determination, which she did not understand. Edgar's life assured him of a place in the kingdom of heaven.

I have my penance to pay.

Sugar had to receive her truth from me. Thomas tied me to never reveal his paternity. How was I going to do this? My great-grandson was the key that triggered the unlocking of my secret past. I had much to ponder and honour, even in death.

MY PROBLEMS MOUNTED when Mrs Biswas's younger sister, Maureen from the Transvaal, moved into our family home with her sister. Thankfully, I had moved my mother's chest to my section of the house, as she requested before she passed.

Maureen was inquisitive and appeared at my door unannounced. I was on my guard whenever I opened my mother's journals, but one morning while I was in the bathroom, she entered my section of our conjoined home. The interleading door remained unlocked for my mother's easy access.

Chiddy never complained about this arrangement, yet he only ever used the front entrance to my parent's home. Communal living compromised our privacy when Mrs Biswas moved in. She kept away but stirred my father a fair bit to rattle us with her demands.

When my father passed, Maureen set up home with her sister. This led to an added level of interference. Privacy evaporated the day I found her sitting on my lounge room couch.

'Maureen! How did you get in?'

'The side door was open, so I let myself in. You seem to be busy with all those books and papers on the dining room table.'

My heart somersaulted, and I coughed to clear my throat.

Had she read anything on the table?

'Please don't use the side door. I prefer people letting me know when they are coming over.'

'Come on, Milly, do I have to? I'm your step-aunt after all?'

Her audacity made me cringe, and I was not letting her get away with what she had done.

'Please respect my wishes.'

'So, tell me, what's with the paperwork? Are you working now at this stage of your life?'

I ignored her question and offered her a cup of tea. She declined.

'I must get back to my sister. She is unwell, and I'm here to help her, but I get bored on this plantation. How strange it must seem to you to have been born here and still live on this property!'

'I enjoy the peacefulness,' before you arrived, I thought.

That was a narrow escape. She had not read the

journals, is what I had to believe. I wished Edgar was still alive to put a lock on the interleading door. We relied on him for everything.

Mrs Biswas was too frail to come prying into my business. Her children kept away. They got all they ever wanted from my father, and I let that be. George kicked up a fuss, and James did not care. He enjoyed his simple, lonely life. After reading ma's journal about her past, I understood James' silent, distant nature. My father knew James was not his son and made his preference between the boys obvious. I feel intense sadness acknowledging this, and wish I had poured more family love on my older brother. How does any parent, biological or not, do this to a child?

Fate has reared his ugly head. Candace is in a situation that has been misinterpreted. My fallibility has touched Jadon. Not a sin. To love and be loved is never that. But the truth will hurt my Candy girl. Sugar endured much growing up in a racially divided society. I'm hoping I'm right in thinking she will be strong. Nothing will change in the love she shared with Chiddy—the only father she knew.

I'm caught between my secret and the truth that needs to be told. Should I seek Pastor Madlala for advice? Swimming between options heightens the dilemma clanging in my head. If only I could be at the sea, but today I am more willing than able. A sign of how to proceed is necessary. Carrying a lone burden is no way to live. I am a lie to my daughter and granddaughter. How could I have deluded myself that I would never be in this situation? Candy girl must be freed from the horrible situation born from the birth of her beautiful boy. I could edit how much of the truth I revealed.

Did I want to continue living under the veil of deception?

Another fretful night followed many. My peace arrived when Thomas came to me in a dream.

We were sitting on the rock, our love rock. Thomas was as I remembered him. I was haggard. He held my face and whispered in my ear.

'Tell Sugar and Candace about our love. That is all that needs to be said. It will free you—not alter the love they have for you. Trust that, my love.'

I awoke with calm determination. I had to read my mother's remaining journals, and complete my letter to Candace. The journals and my letter must be mailed soon to Sugar and Candace. Mother and daughter deserved the truth. My mother left me her truth. I will ensure that Sugar shares my letter and the journals with Zola. She will never ask, but should know her truth too.

I now understand Zola's need for solitude. She was an introspective child. Quite different from the daring, outgoing, Sugar. I believe she sensed the hidden truths in our family. It is impossible to live a lie and think it will remain unnoticed. My relationship with Chiddy was a sign to my daughters that I did not love him.

They had no reason to question that because Chiddy was a good father to both Sugar and Zola. I never knew his thoughts, only his heart. He loved me.

I picked up my mother's third journal marked, *Milly's Big Day* and a floodgate of tears smudged the echoes of her heart.

I had to protect Milly. Her fate would be worse than mine in this country ruled by racial segregation. She must forgo the love she feels and holds within her. It is a steep price to pay. I have known that for all my married years. I was foolish in thinking I was sparing disgracing my family's name and honour by accepting the elopement offer from a man who did not know what love meant. I did for Milly what my mother had no opportunity to do for me. I chose her husband. A man who would love and cherish her even though she could not return the same to him. How could she? Her heart was stolen and locked. The key remained with the love she could not have again as she desired.

I could not bear that Milly's big day was the saddest day of her life. The sad truth was that marriage was the only way I knew how to protect her. She has been a dutiful daughter. Her heart's calling is not a judgement of her character. She saw through race and dared to claim her once in her lifetime song of love.

I pray every day that she forgives me for steering her life's course. Her sadness dwelled in her eyes. I cooked for the wedding guests as atonement for what I had done to my daughter. Arnold was pleased with the dishes I prepared because Mr Sherman enjoyed them. We pandered to these people to keep a roof over our heads and food on the table. I hope my grand-children are destined for much more. Milly will be trapped on the plantation. The outside world will judge her firstborn. My Milly is a good, kind woman, and that she was brave to know love, although fleeting, makes me happy. The prayer on my lips remains for her safety and happiness, and

I know Edgar will watch over her like a big brother.

My mother's presence loomed over me in those words, as though she were stroking my head and letting me know she loved me. She could never articulate those three magical words I craved to hear her say. Thomas assured me I was loved, and now my mother confirmed what I longed to know.

My light-headedness, and palpitations increased. I put it down to the anxiety of reading through the journals that spoke without fear from my mother's grave. She could never articulate her truth. Now I had to make peace with Candy girl. Sugar and her daughter were about to confront family truths for the first time together. Perspiration saturated my scalp. I lay back on the couch and took a few deep breaths. I dozed off into a memory that emerged in a vivid dream of the day my mother's private life was questioned. There was a gentle knocking on our front door at 10 am on a Thursday. My father was away at a cane growers' meeting. My mother and I were alone in the house. Edgar had gone to the market to pick up a box of vegetables. My mother opened the door to three ladies from the church. Ladies she knew from sight rather than association.

'Good morning, Romola, I hope we have not called at an awkward time.'

'Please come in. It's lovely to see you all. To what do I owe this honour of your surprise visit?' My mother could be quite articulate when my father was out of earshot.

The ladies stepped into our lounge room, and my mother offered them tea.

'Milly, please set up the tea tray. Edgar is out this morning running a few errands.' She felt it was necessary to let the ladies know we were alone in the house.

'The reason for our visit is because we are concerned that you have not attended church for several weeks. Is everything going well here at home?'

The question unnerved my mother, and she fell into a brief silence.

'Our concern is whether Arnold is treating you well. We know cultural expectations can weigh on your shoulders.'

'I don't understand what you mean by that, sister.'

The woman speaking glanced over at the other two ladies, and all three nodded.

'We would like to see you in church on Sundays. Will you return this week?'

'I can't promise that I will, but I might if it's possible.'

The conversation delved further into my parent's relationship.

'Is all well in your marriage, Romola?'

My mother was not letting them into her private

life. She knew they suggested they knew about Mrs Biswas.

'Arnold and I are just fine. He is a good father and husband, so please don't worry on my account. I will attend church when I can. I pray every day and am at peace with that.'

I listened with my ears close to the dining-room doorway, and brought in the tea tray at that moment. My mother had to be saved from explaining her private life to women who never called on her before. They were out to gossip about Mrs Biswas and my father.

'Thank you, Milly. Please sit and join us in tea.' My strategic mother knew how to abort the ladies' agenda. Soon they were on their merry way.

I was proud of my mother's ability to shut down destructive conversations that tarnished reputations and relationships. If only she could do the same with my father and George.

Deep within, she possessed a hidden ethereal courage that surfaced when she was away from my father and brothers.

Only I witnessed when she sat under the cluster of pecan trees in our yard, reading or tending to the nuts, and sometimes staring up at the trees. Her oneness with nature was when she was most serene, close to her beloved trees. It was as though she sat with a friend who understood her thoughts.

Her love for the pecan trees stood like a protective

giant over her, bringing her good favour with her pecan tarts, and fresh nuts, shelled to perfection, ready for eager mouths. Ma's apple pecan crumble pie with a pecan topping made it a finger-licking favourite delight. I could never replicate her pecan pie. The memory is a vivid gustatory delight.

An unseen woman of many virtues with a stifled voice.

I needed to summon the strength she had, to help me cope with Sugar's and my Candy girl's reactions to what I was to expose to them. I cannot travel to Australia to face them in unveiling my life's burden. My health has declined in recent years, and Dr Kelly said I had an irregular heartbeat perhaps caused by some underlying stress. He advised that I avoid physical exertion. Weakness is a sign of shame. I must own my truth and set it free in the universe by being honest with my daughters and granddaughter. The time has come. Blessed with a wonderful family, my profound regret was not being truthful with Chiddy. He deserved my honesty. Like my mother, I will leave my voice in this letter to Candy girl. Jadon's generation needs the truth as soon as possible.

The day I mailed my letter, with instructions on where to find my mother's journals, I felt lightheaded and tired.

The sequence of how I ended up in the hospital baffles me. I blinked and opened my eyes when I heard someone asking, 'Who is your next of kin, my dear?

We need to contact someone to tell them you cannot return home with no one to take over your care.' A kind-faced nurse smiled down at me.

I told her my granddaughter Candace Law's telephone number was in my address book, in my handbag, on the bedside table. I asked how I got to the hospital.

'There was a call from the local post office that you collapsed at their door as you walked out. An ambulance picked you up and brought you here. Your granddaughter is a long way off. Is there anybody else we can contact here?'

'My daughter Zola's and my son-in-law, Aru's, numbers are in the book.'

I did not want to trouble Zola or Aru and have them know my truth before Sugar and Candy girl had my letter. I must guard my truth until my letter arrives in Australia.

THOUGHTS OF JAMES and his separation from his biological father reverberated with an emotional tug. Jadon cannot live like James did—not knowing his origins, living in the shadows of a life he did not choose. His unknown pain manifested in his serene, haunting flute playing. It was his voice, his chant for freedom from my father's overbearing attitude and the subjugation of his plantation life.

I often wondered how both my brothers were so different. James' pious spirit wafted from the lilting melodies he played, circling our home, music from another world that drove the listener to inexplicable tears. There were days after he and my mother had toiled in the heat on the sugarfields, when he sat with her under the pecan trees, playing her favourite strains. She sat with closed eyes lost in sublime meditative bliss. My father called James a musical weakling, hoping that would stop him playing the flute. I felt a soul searching ache but never bonded with him. He shut me out—remaining mysterious. After reading my mother's journal entries, I felt a closeness with James. He was of her, but not from us. His soul carried the music of the old country and unbeknownst to him a longing for a father he never knew. Perhaps a loving father.

It was up to me to save my great-grandchild from a similar fate.

THE LETTER THOMAS wrote before his death dwells forever. As I lay forlorn in my hospital bed, his words, his face, and his touch were as vivid as the day we met behind the bus shelter. I was awkward and afraid, and he burned with passion.

The day Edgar gave me Thomas' letter—I walked alone on the beach where we met on a few secret dates. I felt Thomas walk beside me. Balmy heat and hot tears stung my salty cheeks. I had an overwhelming urge to scream into the air. All I managed was a whisper proclaiming my undying love for Thomas.

I will carry this into the afterlife.

The same event captured my joy and sadness. I had my once-in-a-lifetime experience. For that, I am grateful.

I found love and had to let it go. Thomas and I had unresolved issues. He chose when to end his earthbound trek. Why? I needed closure or fear I may wander along this beach, forever haunted.

We have much to resolve and have the lives we have yet to live to search for answers, pay our dues, make it right.

In my dream state and now in my waking state, his words linger like a sweet caress, 'We shall meet again, my love.'

<hr>

EDGAR DROVE me home that day, his head bowed, afraid to make eye contact with me.

He said as I got out of the van, 'Miss Milly. You going to be all right.'

PART FIVE

CANDACE

My mother flew back to South Africa when news reached us that grandma Milly had a stroke. We spoke in hushed tones, caught between the sadness of her illness and whether she could gather the information we needed on our lineage. Guilt for the pressure I had placed on my grandmother to deliver on our family history was unbearable. My mother and I departed at the airport, drowning in tears, drenched with our hope and fear. Grandma Milly's health had to take precedence over what Terence wanted.

Two days after my mother left for South Africa, my grandmother's letter arrived in the mail.

Grandma Milly lapsed into a coma before my mother got to her bedside at the hospital. I could not open her letter now. My mother and I had to do this together in conversation with my grandmother.

Terence abandoned us without legitimate reason—he would have to wait on my terms. I had not seen or heard from him in three months. Challenges appeared in a succession of three. Grandma Milly said ill luck came in threes. Here it was, Terence's demand, the pressure I put on my grandmother, and now her illness. Who knows what else life had in store for me? Her letter stared at me from the entrance hall table. I would only read it when she was well again.

My mother summoned her usual fight to insist I read it now to *sort out* my relationship with Terence. I could not tell her I had no intention of reconciling with him. Her heart wanted Jadon to have a present father. This was not on the cards I held! A girl must stand her ground. This could be the unpeeling of one mask, and he might have many more. When a person shows you who they are, you better believe it! My determination to follow through on my decision exuded my maternal fire!

Jadon is the light of my life. I had to focus all my energy on him. He was three months old when my mother rushed back to South Africa. He formed a loving bond with her and was fretful for a few days after her departure. His brightest blue, innocent baby eyes invited trouble. But his smile and the flatness of his feet with Terence's characteristic long big toe confirmed his paternity. Discarded, that's how I felt! How could I have been blind to the nuances of his personality? Nobody does a three hundred-and-sixty-degree turn without some slip-ups on who they truly are. Is love blind? My family loved Terence and did not see this coming. My thoughts, on auto rewind, ate into my soul. I had to get out of the quietness of the house, with my mother away. My mind needed distractions. Jadon was a delightful baby, and everything ran like clockwork on his feeding and change schedule. I strapped Jadon into his baby seat and drove to the office without letting them know I was coming over.

'I wish you told us you were coming in with Jadon. We would have arranged morning tea and a babysitter for a good chat with you. We have missed having you in the office, keeping us calm and focused!'

I heard nothing but the word 'babysitter,' from my office manager, Maryanne.

'A babysitter, why?'

Maryanne looked surprised at my snappy question. She hesitated, not knowing how to respond.

'Just for a bit of you time with us. You need to give yourself a break sometimes. Think about getting a nanny, especially now that your mother is not here to help you. It will make a world of difference. That way you can come into the office one morning a week, or whatever suits you.'

'I have given myself extended maternity leave. That is all I need.'

My flustered behaviour made me concerned that Maryanne might interpret it as depression, or me acting irrationally. A nanny was out of the question.

Terence was the enemy looming in my mind. What if he hurt Jadon? I trembled with that thought.

How could the man I loved so deeply confuse me into not trusting his intentions? It was too soon to leave Jadon with anyone other than my mother. I must have slipped into an awkward silence when I heard Maryanne say Jadon was crying.

'I should head home. Send over any work that might lighten your load. This is a hectic time of the year but it's like this all the time.'

'Stay for a cup of coffee before you leave. I'll tell Louise to pick up your fav apple tart from the bakery downstairs.'

'That sounds tempting, but I must leave, now.'

I rushed out, embarrassed that my fear made me visibly jittery. Thoughts of Jadon being hurt or taken terrified me.

The warm sun soothed my nerves on my walk to the car. Jadon kicked his legs in the air and cooed when he felt the sun on his face.

Nothing but my baby mattered in my world. As a child, I knew the depth of my mother's love for me. She encouraged me to take chances in life and to dare to be different. I wanted the same and more for Jadon.

I was glad to be back in my empty, silent home. It felt safe from prying questions and suggestions about what I needed to do. Maryanne meant well. I understood her concern for me.

Fear is debilitating to a mind that once trusted.

Within an hour of putting Jadon down for his nap, the landline buzzed. I rushed to pick up the call, expecting my mother on the other end.

'Hello. Candace, how are you and my great grandson?'

I controlled the urge to sigh in exasperation. It was Terence's grandmother!

'We are well, thank you.

'You sound surprised to hear my voice. Who were you expecting on the line?'

'Yes, I'm surprised to hear your voice. I am waiting for a call from my mother in South Africa.'

'Oh, she's left you on your own, then.'

'Yes, my grandmother is gravely ill.'

'I'm sorry to hear that. Did you get the information that Terence required?'

Her insensitivity made my stomach churn. All she cared about was what she wanted to know. She was getting no answer from me!

'I really can't talk now. Sorry. I hear Jadon fussing.'

Her protests, 'Candace, hold on, I don't hear the baby crying. Candace, are you there?' died when I plonked the phone down on her.

I flopped on the couch. There was no returning from this, not with Terence, his mother and grandmother.

No matter what grandma Milly revealed in her letter, Terence and his family will never have access to it. I owed them nothing. My family history was not up for public scrutiny.

I jumped up and grabbed grandma Milly's letter from the hallway table, and locked it in my bedside drawer.

I was not ready for the secrets it carried. My energy needed preservation.

WHEN MARYANNE CALLED me from the office, a few days after my visit, I knew something had happened. Her uncertain tone, and whispered voice held fear, different from her usual bold friendliness. Confident Maryanne never displayed this side of herself with me. I relied on her to keep my business running while I tended motherhood and weathered my issues with Terence.

'What's the matter, Maryanne? You sound worried about something.'

'Look, dear, I don't know if it's my place to tell you, but I know if I don't, I will regret it somewhere in time.'

'Are you planning on resigning? Is the work too much? I understand the pressure you're under with staff apathy. Don't stress, I can return to work as soon as possible or employ another person to ease your load.'

I babbled on and heard Maryanne groan.

'No, I'm not leaving. This is a private matter that affects you. So I'm nervous.'

'Really? What have I done?'

'Nothing, that's why I need to tell you. Is there a time we can meet soon?'

'Just say it. I'm hanging on so many issues. Please don't add another noose by making me wait.'

'Er... well... here it is. Terence was out dining at Harbourside last night. He was with a woman. They were hanging onto each other, holding hands, leaning on each other. It was obvious they were dating. I hope I have not overstepped the line by telling you.'

I paused, digested, and reacted.

'This is no surprise. He walked out on Jadon and me and thinks he's a free man now. Thank you for letting me know. You have given me another valid reason to do what I must do. Something I must act on right away.'

'Please carefully consider your line of action. What if this is a passing fling?'

'All the more reason to act in the heat, my dear Maryanne. Thank you. We'll pretend we did not have this conversation.'

'Are you sure about this? If you need any help outside of the office, please let me know.'

'Thank you, I will. Promise me you won't worry about anything, and I trust you will hold this information close.'

'Absolutely. My lips are sealed. You amaze me, Candace. Here you are worrying about me.'

'I am my grandmother's granddaughter!' I guffawed.

Maryanne made me promise we would meet for coffee soon.

I had to seek legal advice. I did not need counselling. Terence has moved on with *his* life—without *his* son. I was sad for my baby, but Maryanne's revelation did not affect me.

What she revealed might not hold up legally. The restaurant would have footage to prove his infidelity. Added to his abandonment of our young family, this gave me the upper hand. Privacy laws might protect him because he had not technically committed a crime.

Four days after grandma Milly slipped into a coma, she passed early on that Friday morning. My father called me with the sad news. He and aunt Zola were taking care of the funeral arrangements.

'Your mother is blaming herself for not being here with grandma Milly. She is not sleeping and is exhausted. I know once you arrive, she will feel better.'

'Get ma some sleeping pills. She must rest. The flight would have exhausted her, too. I will fly over as soon as possible. I suppose it's too soon to ask what day we will hold the funeral.'

'Your mother is as stubborn as she is lovable. She

refuses to take any sleeping pills. She might listen to you. We expect the funeral will be Friday week.'

'I'll get things arranged here, but dread having to ask Terence to sign consent for me to travel to South Africa with Jadon. The child he disowned!'

'Candace, pull yourself together, do what needs to be done. You don't want to jeopardise things with Terence.'

I held my tongue to avoid riling my father. He believed this was a temporary impasse between Terence and me. He adored his masked son-in-law.

I had twenty-four hours to call Terence and book our airline tickets. I hated the irony of getting consent from him.

His mobile phone rang out a few times before he answered my call.

'Candace! This is a surprise. Do you have the news I'm waiting for?'

'No, Terence, grandma Milly has passed, and I have to travel to South Africa with Jadon.'

What he said sealed our irreconcilable marriage.

'Sorry about grandma Milly. That stuffs up the chance of you securing the information I need.'

With my hand over my mouth, I smothered the exhalation of my anger at his crass expectation. I could not mess up getting his signed consent to have Jadon travel with me. It's not like he cared!

'Grandma Milly has left documents on our family history. I will look through them in South Africa.'

'Great to know she had the foresight to understand the urgency of the matter. I will get the consent document signed right away. Condolences to your family.'

He hung up without asking how his son was doing. Not a word about how my mother was taking the loss of grandma Milly. She doted on Terence, ensuring he was happy, comfortable, and well-fed! This added to a long list of why we would never be a couple or a family.

Jadon and I flew to South Africa on Monday afternoon. My father met us at the airport and drove us to the plantation.

'Are we all staying at the plantation home this week, pa?'

'We are gathering there today, but you and Jadon will stay at our home. Your son will get to sleep in your old bedroom. You know somewhere in time we shall talk to him about this.'

'I wish grandma Milly could have been around Jadon as he grows.'

'We cannot plan our exit, darling. All we have is now.'

My wise father made me see the rational side of life and death. His pragmatism did not sit well with many. I prepared myself for the emotional meeting with aunt Zola and my mother, but had to be strong for them. Grandma Milly was the last of her generation in our small family.

Aunt Zola met me on the front porch. She

embraced me with her penetrating soft eyes, which bathed me in her calm aura.

Her hug lasted a little longer than usual. My aunt remained tranquil throughout our family's highs and lows.

'Sugar is asleep. She has exhausted herself with relentless crying after she went through ma's belongings. A host of photographs, and a letter left on her bedside table included how she wished to be farewelled. Sugar's blaming herself for not being home when ma took ill. Hopefully, she will feel better now that you're here.'

Gracious aunt Zola, stoic as always, just as grandpa Chiddy carried himself through life. She asked for nothing in her silent presence. If only I could be like her. Reactive defined the younger me, but I'm working on what I secretly call 'Zolafying' myself.

'I won't wake her. I'll settle Jadon and unpack. Please let me know what I can do to help with the funeral. You've been shouldering this on your own.'

'It's just good to have you here. Your father wasted no time in arranging the funeral. He is our pillar. I must complete the speakers' list. Ma left a list of requests in her letter, so we'll follow that. I'll leave you to arrange that if that's ok.'

'Absolutely. If there's anything else, pass it on to me. You, ma, and pa have been stretched ever since grandma Milly passed. It feels strange thinking and saying she's passed.'

'With your parent's approval, I've arranged for Ruth, Norah's niece, to help you with Jadon. You remember her? She's Beatrice's daughter.'

'I do. She will be good with Jadon.'

It felt strange being in my grandparent's home without either of them there. My father was right. We never know when our exit from life will be called. It was a certainty. The precise hour is beyond human control.

Aunt Zola prepared breakfast, and Ruth arrived to help me with Jadon's care. My fear that someone might hurt or take Jadon from me, faded. The fear was related to Terence. This comforted me that I was not losing my mind. I have always been my worst critic. It must have something to do with being an only child.

My mother rose around noon, showered, and came out to greet me. Her chalk-white skin worried me. In a matter of days, she appeared run down and frail. I watched her steady herself on the chair before she sat down.

'How are you, ma? We are together now for me to take care of you.' I smiled, hoping it would lighten the grief she felt.

'Who said I needed care? I'm ok. Jadon, needs your attention. We arranged Ruth to assist you. Are you happy with that?'

'Thank you for that, ma. Yes, I'm happy you did. Let's take a walk in the garden. I could use some fresh air. How about you?'

'That will be good. I'm so glad you are here with Jadon. I worried Terence would not consent to you travelling out of the country with the baby.'

'Nothing to worry about on that score. He's given up on us, and from what I hear, he's moved on too.'

'So be it. You have much to celebrate about you. It is his loss. We wish him well.'

'Yep! We will put all our energy in laying grandma Milly to rest.'

'I'm struggling with the pressure I put on her to get our family origins verified. I fear that escalated her pressure, then the stroke.' She stopped and stared out across the plantation, which was no longer recognisable with technological advancement in the last decade.

'It's a burden we both carry, but as pa said, we don't know when we will be called to our rest.'

'Have you told your father what grandma Milly was doing for us?'

'No, we didn't get around to that. She might have told him when he called to check on her while you were in Australia helping me.'

'Perhaps. There has been no time to talk to him about those matters.'

'Let it be for now. A few days after the funeral, we will read grandma Milly's letter, and go through all the memorabilia she has gathered.'

'Please, let's go somewhere else to read her letter. I couldn't bear doing that in her home.'

'Yes, that's the best way. Allow me to arrange it with aunt Zola. She must be with us when we read the letter.'

'I agree. We need to support each other through whatever comes to light. Please don't arrange a restaurant or coffee shop. This is a small town that will gossip about our heartlessness over my mother's passing.'

'Perhaps a walk in the park or the beach. We can settle on the place later.'

I left my mother sitting in the garden and walked back to the house to assist aunt Zola. She watched us from the kitchen window. When I suggested the three of us should go to a park or the beach for a quiet time, a day or two after the funeral, she stared, nodded and walked away.

My grandmother's home overflowed with mirth whenever we visited her—now it was a silent marbled mausoleum of muted memories.

My grandmother left explicit instructions for her last rites. She wanted to be cremated and her ashes scattered at her favourite beach. A niggling thought crept in. Did she decide the day of her final rest her? Had my demands pushed her over the edge?

My father wrote a beautiful eulogy on grandma Milly. Her father and brothers paid her no homage in life, but her son-in-law cherished her like his own.

I shared my memories of the grandmother who was everything rolled into one—teacher, sister, friend, grandmother. At her request, the dirge at her crema-tion was *Ave Maria.*

All her requests made perfect sense after we read her letter. She found her absolution from the lifelong burden she carried. But she loved, knew love, felt loved, and claimed brief happiness that carried her through to her passing.

———

TWO DAYS after grandma Milly's funeral, aunt Zola, my mother, and I drove to her favourite beach with her ashes. We sat on the shore, hands intertwined and meditated in the bliss of sunrise. A beam of light flick-ered over her brass urn, making her presence palpable. Then, beginning with my mother, her eldest daughter, we read a page from her detailed letter. It was a thick wad of floral paper secured with a pink ribbon. Her pages were intact as we read her heartfelt outpourings of her life, love, and loss. She spared no detail. It was as though she was sitting in the centre of the circle, right on the spot where we had placed her urn.

There were no tears, just a warm understanding that we knew her—authentically her.

Great-grandfather Arnold stained our family with his violent past.

Albert Sherman controlled our family through to grandma Milly's generation. Her heart revealed to us on the day her ashes floated into the sea, confirmed her return to her beloved mother, grandpa Chiddy, and Thomas. My mother is the striking candle of their union. I am so proud of the strong woman my grandmother was. My mother's eyes were dewy, not sad, as she came to terms with the story of her birth.

She whispered, 'I'm blessed to have had two fathers. Never forget,' she said with a crack in her voice and a sideways glance at me, 'grandpa Chiddy was the best father any girl could ever have.'

She reached for aunt Zola's hand and both nodded. Aunt Zola looked at me first, then my mother, and said, 'Sugar, we also had the best mother any girl could ask for.'

My mother released aunt Zola's hand from her clasp, and both hugged. They were blood sisters, united by their mother, and nothing could take that away from them. We strolled down to the water's edge, waded in waist-high and set grandma Milly free.

As her ashes floated on calm waters, we tossed red rose petals. We watched them swirl in long hoops as she drifted further out on sun tipped sparkling ripples and disappeared. I heard my mother whisper into the wind with her eyes closed, 'Thank you, ma, I will always love you.'

A breeze fluttered, breaking the still morning to acknowledge and return our love.

There was much to do to tie up my grandmother's affairs. The first being the title deeds, to the plantation house, left in my mother's name. Thomas Sherman's final acknowledgment of his daughter. Grandma Milly wrapped the letter from Thomas in her pink silk scarf. He instructed her on who to contact for the handing over of the property to my mother.

I mulled over the situation without verbalising that Thomas had probably intended for his daughter to inherit everything once grandma Milly passed. There was no record of this in my grandmother's letters. She loved her daughters equally and carried the burden of her past with her. Grandma Milly entitled both her daughters to all that was hers.

She was an upstanding moral woman. Nobody could say anything to the contrary.

We set aside another day to read my great-grandmother's journals. Grandma Milly wanted us to read it together.

As a family of women—we were strong. Nothing could shake us.

We spent many nights going through great-grandma Romola's journals. That great-grandfather was capable of murder was shocking and hard to digest. I left it to hearsay.

Nobody wants to know this or ever acknowledge such a horrible family history. I looked at Jadon and knew that he must never be told this dark secret.

My grandmother knew love as life's greatest asset. I drew inspiration from that. Terence loved me once, but the women in his life, with their Lady Macbeth machinations, altered his heart and mind. That was the only thing I struggled to comprehend. I had to release my anger. Sadness will never undo me. I have my son who, like my mother, was born of love. That is what I had to believe.

I LEFT for Australia clear on my purpose and a heart that was much lighter than it had been in recent months. My life was before me, and as my pa said, I will live in the now.

When I arrived on Australian shores, I was more determined than ever to process my divorce. My life needed attention. I had to make my presence felt at the office if I expected my business to run smoothly.

As a single parent, I had to be successful to ensure Jadon had the life I hoped to give him. We did not need a penny from Terence in child support. It is hypocritical to expect this from someone who did not show up for his newborn son. My mother offered to return to Australia once grandma Milly's estate was settled, and aunt Zola had moved into the plantation home. I left that up to the sisters to decide, although I felt it should be aunt Zola's decision on where she lived. My mother was headstrong, wanting things done her way.

For the first time, I felt alone in Sydney. An aching aloneness that caught me by surprise. My mind wandered back and forth to grandma Milly's letter and the life she had lived. Sleeplessness left me fatigued. My lawyer assured me the divorce would run as planned. Cut and dried. There could be no issues in a case of parental abandonment of a newborn child. The annoying thing was I had to prove Terence's paternity, as that was his bone of contention. Why? News was out that he had moved on, had a new woman hanging onto him. My mind played havoc with my life again. I had to get out of the house. After an exhausting overthinking night, the morning was radiant enough for a drive to Bondi for a beach walk with Jadon. We both needed some sea air. More me than Jadon. He slept through the night, had a good appetite and his rosy cheeks proved he was thriving.

I planned a brisk walk, but with the baby in a stroller, it was not that easy. The Bondi Beach walkway was quiet without the usual throngs of people during weekends. Jadon enjoyed the warmth of the sun and cooed with delight.

My body was relaxed, but my mind continued to dance around my grandmother, Terence, and the nature of Thomas Sherman's death. I sat on a bench to take a meditative moment to still my thoughts. The sea had a hypnotic effect on me. In the depths of my reverie, I heard a voice say, 'Excuse me, sorry to bother you...'

I snapped back to being present and looked into the startling green eyes of a lovely, smiling young woman.

'Oh, sorry, I did not see you there. I was deep in thought. How may I help you?'

'I peeped into your stroller when I heard your baby cooing, then I saw his gorgeous face. I wanted to tell you that you have a beautiful baby.'

I looked at Jadon and smiled. 'This lovely lady says you're a gorgeous boy, Jadon.'

The woman and I laughed

'I love his name. May I hold him?'

I hesitated for a second and felt silly for being overprotective. 'Sure, I'll pick him up for a brief cuddle. We must get home soon; we have a long way to go.'

That is all I remember until I woke up inside an ambulance.

'My baby, where's my baby?' I cried, tugging at the paramedic sitting beside me.

'Please remain calm. You received a blow to the back of your head. The police will talk to you. They are on their way to the hospital. You might need a few stitches.'

'I want my baby. Where is he?' I tried to sit up to get a glimpse of Jadon.

'You must sit still. We are almost at the hospital.'

'Please let me see my boy?'

'We don't have your baby. We received a call from a man living in an apartment block across from where you were attacked. Perhaps the police will let you speak to him.'

'Attacked? By whom?'

My head ached. I felt queasy and weak. I was alone with no backup to help me through this terrible ordeal. My handbag sat next to me. I reached for my mobile phone.

Who would I call? I paused, hoping it would clear my mind to think about what I had to do. I had to keep calm, but my suppressed emotions passed through my lips in uncontrollable sobs.

Two police officers were in attendance while I was being triaged in the emergency department. Thankfully, I did not need stitches for the superficial head wound I received.

The officers approached me in a private enclosed space and asked if I was up to answering a few questions. I nodded.

'My baby, will you find my baby?'

'Your baby is our priority, madam. We need you to remember everything you can to help us find the child. According to your driver's license, you live a fair distance from the beach for a morning stroll. What made you come this way?'

'I love this beach and brought my baby here for his first visit. It was our outing after our overseas trip.'

'Overseas trip?' The officer frowned.

'Yes, we've recently returned from a close family member's funeral in South Africa, and I thought a walk here would be good for us. For me, really.'

I said more than I should have. All that mattered was finding Jadon.

'Is there anyone we could call to be with you now, perhaps the baby's father or a family member?'

This question exacerbated how alone I was in this moment.

'No, no family. I'm separated from my husband.'

The police officers gave each other a knowing nod. Their non-verbal communication judged me. It would be the basis in their investigation on who took Jadon.

'Would the baby's father have any reason to take the child?'

My dirty linen was about to be aired. I did nothing wrong, but felt responsible for the situation I was in.

'No, no, not at all. He abandoned the baby at birth. He had no reason to do that.'

'Does anybody else have a reason to abduct your baby?'

'What is that supposed to mean?' The word 'abduct' had an ominous ring. I was ready to run back to the beach to look for Jadon.

'Just routine questions, Mrs Laws. It's a process of elimination of suspects.'

My chest constricted, I struggled to breathe. The words, 'abduct' and 'suspect' were words I never imagined would be applied to my life. The police did not know where to look for Jadon, and I was no help without a clue on why anyone would take my child.

'We could drive you home to get some rest and return tomorrow with any leads on the investigation.'

How did an innocent morning with my baby

become an investigation? I was living my worst nightmare, and could not call my parents, not now.

'Please, I don't want to go home,' I sobbed. 'I would rather walk along the beach looking for my baby.'

'That is not a good idea. Leave it to us. We need some photographs of the baby, tell us what he was wearing and describe his stroller. That would help us a lot.'

I could not focus with my head in a muddled fog. Nothing came to mind. I could not even remember if Jadon had his blue outfit on or whether I packed his blue outfit in his bag and dressed him in the yellow romper. My stress levels were high and because my blood pressure soared, the doctor on duty advised that I spend the night in hospital. I was a mess—a sobbing hindrance to the police. The older police officer sat next to me, pitying my heightened anxiety.

'One more question, please, Mrs Laws. Did your husband have visitation rights with the child?'

I felt incriminated by the question and had to consider how I framed my response to avoid sounding like a bitter, jilted wife. How was I going to mention the paternity test Terence requested without attaching a negative image to myself? This information was lucid, but the details of my beach walk remained hazy.

'He chose not to see his child. I know he would not do this.'

'May we have your husband's address to let him

know what has happened and question him to assess if he can lead us to who has the baby?'

'How would he know? May I accompany you to see Terence, please?'

'The doctor has advised that you remain here overnight. How about we do this in the morning?'

'But should we not find Jadon today? What if the person who has taken him leaves the country?'

'All in good time, Mrs Laws. We have already sent out an APB about your baby's abduction. Whoever took him cannot leave the country without being apprehended.'

I found that hard to believe, but had no choice.

I tossed and turned that night, searching for answers. It was my negligence in slipping into my thoughts, daydreaming about our family situation in South Africa, that made me careless. At the crack of dawn, I called my lawyer. All he said after listening to my lengthy explanation of the day's events was that he would contact the police officers who questioned me. Here I was, stuck in limbo! He suggested I call Terence before Jadon's disappearance hit the television news. I could not do this alone. I waited for the police officers to arrive and left with them at noon to see Terence. The police called to tell him they were coming over to discuss a matter they could not disclose on the phone, and he agreed to meet them at his home.

Terence was alone in his apartment. His frown and

darting eyes conveyed his shock at seeing me flanked by two police officers.

'What's going on, Candace?'

I blurted out, 'Somebody has taken Jadon. I took him to Bondi...'

He searched the police officer's faces, was silent, unperturbed, but turned his gaze on me and asked, 'Taken? By whom?'

'I don't know,' I sobbed.

'Mrs Laws, you must remain calm if you want to be here whilst we question your husband.'

'I'm sorry...'

'I hope you don't think I took the child. Candace, you know I would never do that.'

'Yes, I said that to the officers.'

After a series of questions about who was likely to take the child, a disgruntled client or neighbour, the police asked if Terence was in a relationship with anyone. He cleared his throat, threw me a furtive glance, oozing with guilt, and asked for a private conversation with the questioning officer. He declined the privilege. Finding Jadon was paramount, and time was running out.

'Lily and I broke off our brief relationship two days ago.' I got another guilt-laden look from Terence.

'Two days ago,' both police officers spoke in unison.

'Yes, but she would have no cause to take Jadon.

Her anger is against me for breaking off our relationship.'

'A brief relationship, you say. How brief?'

'Three months, on and off.'

'Then, it's fair to say you don't know Lily that well.'

Silence.

'You don't know her well enough to attest to her character, is that correct?'

'Please answer the question, Mr Laws.'

'Yes, I suppose...'

'What line of work is she in?'

Terence stared at the worn rug on the floor.

'She's a waitress at Bondi Pavilion.'

'When were you going to tell us that, Mr Laws? Do you have a photograph of Lily?' The senior officer lost his cool, raising his voice and glaring at Terence.

Terence pulled out his phone from his pants pocket. Looming as his screensaver was the startling green eyes of a smiling, lovely young woman.

'That's her! She is the woman who stopped to speak to me and asked to hold Jadon before I blacked out.'

'Blacked out?' Terence asked.

'Yes, Mr Laws, your wife was attacked at Bondi Beach yesterday. She received a blow to the back of her head and spent the night in hospital.'

'Right.' Terence placed his hand on his chin and looked down at the worn rug again. He made no comment on the officer's explanation of what had happened to me.

The questioning officer asked Terence to accompany them to Lily's place, but he did not want to be involved. I pleaded with the senior officer to allow me to go with them to her place.

'You must stay in the vehicle for the baby's safety. If we need you, we will ring you to come out. Is that clear?'

'Do you think Jadon is with her?'

'We're about to find out, aren't we?'

I had to hold my tongue to avoid irritating the officers.

Lily lived in Ramsgate with her grandmother. That's as much as Terence could tell us.

The police vehicle parked a street away from the house. This could be tricky if her grandmother was in the house. After an agonising five minutes, the senior officer sent me a text message.

> We can hear a baby crying inside the house. Step out of the car and wait for my next message.

When the younger officer called, I heard a woman protesting in the background that she was babysitting for her granddaughter's friend.

'Hurry over, Mrs Laws, we think the baby is yours.'

I ran like one chased by a pack of wild wolves, tripping, almost falling on the pebbled laneway. My heart pounded as I raced up the driveway. I heard Jadon's cry and called out, 'I'm coming, baby, I'm coming.'

A white-haired woman, still in her nightgown at 2 pm, stood at the door with Jadon in her arms, refusing to let him go.

'No, you can't take the baby. He's my granddaughter's friend's child. I'm helping her babysit him while she's at work. I'll be in a lot of trouble if I give you the baby. Please call her at work first.'

'Hand over the baby. This is his mother.'

The senior officer told his partner to call for backup. They planned to confront Lily at work. Backup police would watch that the old lady did not alert Lily to what had happened. Terence was called and asked to sit tight at home until they questioned Lily.

'There will be a lot more trouble for you, madam, if you don't return the child to his mother.'

The old woman reluctantly handed Jadon to me. He was clean, but his flushed face and dry mouth conveyed his obvious stress as he seemed to have been crying for a long spell. I clutched him close against my chest. He stopped crying when he heard my voice.

'Mrs Laws, a taxi will arrive shortly to take you and the baby home. I'm arranging for a doctor to call at the house to have a look at the baby. On no account must you leave the house. We will locate the stroller and gather more information and see you later today.'

'Thank you...thank you so much.'

All I wanted was to go home.

Lily was in police custody that afternoon.

Terence called to say he was sorry that things turned out this way, and asked if I would consider seeing him once things had settled down. I was not keen to see him and knew he wanted the matter cleared on my ancestry. Jadon was unharmed. That was all I cared about. I called my parents, who were distraught by what had transpired.

'I will be with you in a few days, Candace. This is shocking! Your father will come over a week after me.'

'Please don't rush things, ma, I am well, as is Jadon. Do what you must do there first.'

'It's settled, Candace. I will call with the day and time of my arrival.'

Nobody could tell my mother what to do when her mind was made up.

I AGREED to meet Terence when my mother arrived in Sydney. It was something I preferred to avoid, but knew it was necessary given all that had happened. I refused to go to his apartment but agreed to meet at an outdoor coffee shop closer to my home. It was a chilly night. It was an uncomfortable meeting. I hated confrontation. We had never argued prior to Jadon's birth.

'Candace, please believe me when I say I'm really sorry for what Lily put you and Jadon through.'

'It is done now, although there is a court hearing to face, so when I say it's done... Jadon and I are over the hardest part. I have my son back.'

An awkward silence penetrated the cold night air. My coffee grew cold, but I had to address the pink elephant between us.

'About that paternity test you require.' He looked up at me and shook his head.

'We don't have to talk about that now.'

'We do, Terence. It destroyed our marriage. My mother is of mixed race. Grandpa Chiddy was not her biological father. Hence Jadon's blue eyes and light hair. My mother found out after grandma Milly passed.'

Silence.

'I do not want a DNA test done on Jadon. My mother will do a test to prove to you who her father was. Hence, your son is of mixed race. It's not me sleeping around! How does that sit with you?'

Terence stared at me, mute for once in his life. I held the trump card now, and he had to prove whether he could be man enough to accept what I laid before him. How dare he even assume infidelity on my part when all I did was work my butt off in the five years of our marriage?

'I believe what you say.... There's no need for Sugar to prove anything to me. Did grandma Milly have an affair or was she raped?'

Every blood vessel in my body was ready to

explode! The audacity, the hide, the downright cheek to expect me to dignify his sordid question!

'Do you honestly expect an answer? My mother was born from love. That is all you need to know. I must go now.' I rose with a sudden jerk. My chair screeched across the concrete floor.

'Why did we have to meet to have this conversation? If you have any further questions, either email me or send me a text message. I must go. My son needs me.' I turned and walked away.

'Candace, please wait. I did not mean to upset you. I have an important question. Please give me five minutes.'

'The answer is, yes again and again, Jadon is your son, if that's what you want to ask.' I called out from where I stood.

'No, that's not it. Do you think we can work things out between us? Please, Candace. I made a terrible mistake.'

I glared at him, stepped back to the table and whispered in a low menacing voice, 'Mistake? Are you kidding me? You know the answer to that. Good night, Terence. See you in court.'

'I will sign the papers, I promise.'

I trudged home on this freezing night, hot tears scalded my cheeks as I mumbled a prayer for him to honour his word. He was the one begging. It was a wasted performance.

There was no return to the way we were.

I GOT my divorce from Terence without a hitch. He asked to be allowed to see Jadon once a month for a brief visit with either my mother or me present. I reluctantly agreed.

My mother never disclosed to him who her father was. Sugar was Sugar, nobody made her do what she did not have to do.

When I look back at her ancestry, she has a touch of Albert Sherman in her. He controlled our family down to our names. Jadon broke that cycle. My mother exerted control over others. It was the power of her argument, reasoning, or lack of comment that was her secret weapon to survive. She made her voice heard— no matter the outcome.

What Terence did not count on was how awkward every visit with Jadon would be with my mother present. She loved fiercely and disliked with equal intensity.

My mother adored Terence, once, and did everything to keep him happy. That was no longer required in her book. Her rule book had three strikes and out you go! Terence got one from me, or perhaps Lily was the second nail!

Lily had her court hearing, and by Australian law, had to serve a ten-year prison sentence. I suspected her time would be reduced for affectations of good behaviour—never wrongfully accused. Lily had to have a few rocks rolling around her head to do what she did. Terence might have had a few dancing in his head too. He chose her. There was no way that I was ever going to reconsider our relationship. Not after what he put *his child* through.

I am part Sherman. Nobody messes with that.

———

TRUTH AND TIME are angels of the virtuous.

PART SIX

SUGAR

I knew I was different. I felt it deep within me. The pallor of my skin never mattered to me. There was a yearning to be more, much more than the plantation life I was born into. This gave rise to my teenage wildness. I put my mother through a great deal of angst. She was a strict adherent of propriety—keeping up appearances. I had to be me, although I did not have a clear understanding of what I expected of myself. My mother's protection of image and dignity must have stemmed from the dehumanising impact of segregation. I had no fear or respect for it. Nobody could undermine my self-worth. My father Chiddy let me do as I pleased. His silence balanced my mother's tongue on my wayward behaviour. I loved the cultural bond my family had, but I had a fascination for how the other side of town, the privileged, segregated white population lived.

Albert Sherman, in my eyes, was more Indian than white. What with all the food my grandmother cooked for him! Spices galore that made him perspire from every orifice. What a hideous, inerasable sight!

Cultural stories passed down to Zola and me with ease in our conversations with our mother. I never considered myself anything else other than being Chiddy's and Milly's daughter. What you know is what you know. I had no reason to question why Zola and I were different in looks and manner. My mother treated us equally and spoke of how her father showered more love on her brothers. He held uncle George in greater favour over uncle James. All my mother ever said about him was that he was a complicated man.

Once she told me a group of white men beat my grandfather. He stayed on at the pub after Albert Sherman left. Those who watched him had white privilege. They waited for the right moment to beat him to an inch of his life. He was in crutches for three months during which grandma Romola had to bathe him and feed him. His upright gait, his pride, now replaced by a limp. It left him angrier and more vengeful. The incident did not alter his arrogance. My grandmother endured his frequent drunken quarrelsome ways. Albert Sherman sent out his vigilante posse to beat the perpetrators, leaving them maimed with the memory that Arnold was *his man*. Violence bred violence. It surprised my mother that Albert Sherman said it was

God's way, an eye for an eye. Such were the early days of plantation life for migrants. If the white man favoured you, you were a protected species. How could anyone be totally beholden to authority? Now I understand why I am different. Nobody could tame me. I had to be free to run with the wind. Aru accepted me, saying my feisty spirit was what he loved! Candace and I came first in his life. She is a wonderful melding of the both of us. He would sacrifice being called many unmentionables to protect us. Aru and Edgar were similar in their values. My mother said Aru and Edgar were brothers tied by their family values, not blood. Edgar loved hearing her say that whenever she thanked him for helping her with an errand.

I taught kindergarten for two years. When my mother said she and my father would marry me off to halt my wildness, I never told her I was already dating Aru. He was a young man ahead of his time. He valued intelligent women who could hold their own in the world. A man, he said, is not god's gift to women, so why should they be superior? He was my passport to breaking out of the plantation lifestyle and mindset my mother endured.

We enjoyed our early days of marriage, partying, and travelling around South Africa. There were limitations to where we could find accommodation, but good friends in each city we visited gave us a warm bed and a plate of food. We did the same for them.

Unlike my mother, I had a large group of friends, and met other couples that Aru and I befriended through our partying social network. My mother yearned for grandchildren, and Candace brought her great joy. My sister Zola was more like our uncle James, choosing a reclusive life. She has been a wonderful sister and aunt to Candace.

Our family was private. My grandfather bred this value. My mother was an intelligent, friendly being, and I remember her reclusive nature and complete reliance on Edgar. They shared a bond unlike her relationship, or rather the lack of it, with her brothers. His protective nature and watchful eye over her, I most admired. I would tease her and ask why she was so close to Edgar and not Norah. Her reply was always the same.

'You will never understand. You have to experience it to know why.'

Living under the same roof does not allow family the privilege of knowing what lies deep within each member. Sometimes it takes an outsider to know one's true value. My mother's caustic family life with her father and brothers depleted her sense of self. It left her confused about seeking a career, and moving out into the world on her own. Now, the older me wishes I knew everything about her letter and what grandmother's journals exposed.

My darling mother lived with her secret for the

duration of her life. Going through her letter with Candace has somehow left me doubting that she revealed all that she kept hidden for so long. Some unsaid things she took with her to the afterworld. That gnawing thought troubled me, although I respect her right to privacy and am grateful to know how I came to be. Chiddy is my father, the only one I knew. Thomas is now my spiritual father. For that awareness, I'm grateful.

As I sit pondering my mother's love affair, memories of the fleeting times I saw Thomas drive past when I was on my way home from school, or sometimes I saw him at the markets with Edgar. He appeared a kind, quiet man. There was never any conversation, just a smile and raised hand in greeting. I wondered why he was so distant. A conversation with my mother over what I considered strange did not leave my lips in the way I intended. She was at the stove cooking dinner when I touched a nerve.

'Ma, why is Thomas Sherman so unfriendly? He never speaks to me when I see him. He smiles to acknowledge I'm your daughter. Perhaps he is a pervert, leering after the girls he can't have.'

My mother was silent for an eternal five minutes, and when she turned to face me, the look on her face sent fear riveting through my body.

'Listen, Sugar, you may see yourself as a goddess because of your stunning looks, but remember one thing, Thomas Sherman is a gentleman. Never say such things again. Get rid of that horrid pride you carry.' Her voice was a clenched-teeth hiss, quite unlike the time when she chastised me for being responsible for the police visit to our family home.

I knew I had crossed forbidden territory with my mother. She valued humility and appreciated Chiddy and Zola for this.

As I walked away with a mumbled, 'Sorry,' I heard my mother say under her breath, 'You know nothing, to talk like that.' I passed it off as her irritation with me at the time and chose never to mention Thomas Sherman again.

Now, broken pieces fall into place, one memory at a time. How I wish I could tell my mother in the living years I'm happy with how I came to be. I have no shame for being born from such deep love.

I have a secret of my own that is nowhere as deep as the burden my mother and grandmother carried.

My family attributed my reckless partying nights to my rebellious teenage years. Nobody considered I was searching for a lost or unknown sense of self or that I had a boyfriend. Richard was my uptown boy. I used my registered name, Rosalind, and nobody asked questions. He chatted me up at a party, saying he loved my exotic look and that was it. We dated on the condition of my insistence that we avoided being seen together in other public places. Richard enjoyed my mysteriousness, but we lasted for all of six months. There was a disconnect within me I could not fathom. I moved on with Aru my soulmate, and Richard moved to America to pursue his music career. Nobody knows this. Not even Aru.

We hold some things in life close to survive judgement, to allow the self to heal. My mother and I may have had a similar destiny, but I did not love Richard. He was my infatuation with what I could get away with as a child of the plantation.

I hated being born there. Aru was my ticket out of Sherman's Sugar Estate and into a life we defined. He floated into my life quite by chance. Edgar was out running some errands for my mother when the vehicle broke down. Aru drove by and was the only person who offered to assist Edgar. He transported him to our home and Edgar invited him to meet my mother. I opened the front door of our home to Aru that day. The rest is history. We kept the early days of our romance private, but I had no problem convincing my mother he was the one. In her eyes, if he was good enough to assist Edgar, then he qualified for a seat at her table. He made sure he told my parents about his intention to marry me. Pa Chiddy said nothing but nodded and whispered, 'good, good, lovely, lovely' and my mother kissed a rather bashful Aru on the cheek.

One night, before I met Aru, I was at the Beach Hotel party when I saw Albert Sherman's granddaughter, Henry's daughter. I knew her from seeing her at church when we were children. We locked eyes briefly, but there was no acknowledgment that she knew me. If anyone knew that Richard and I were a couple, it would have been her. I often wondered if she alerted the police to my 'illicit' activities. It was a horrid time that frowned upon difference. Love is never an immoral act. The authorities, more particularly the police, made it dirty, an act of sin if love dared stroll across the colour line. It was a sin to divide people by shunting them into racially zoned areas, and creating an unequal education system that disempowered people of colour. I will never know if Henry's daughter sold me out to the police. I feared being called a *coolie* at the social gatherings I attended. It was a stigma-tising social label attached to indentured immigrants.

How would Albert Sherman's granddaughter feel now, knowing I'm her blood relative. Her *coolie* planta-tion cousin? I'm no longer that wild spirit I courted in my younger years who would enjoy saying that to her. When you become a mother, you preserve your fervent desire to protect your child.

As much as I disliked growing up on the planta-tion, I respected the home my parents provided with their limited means. It was a loving home with pa Chiddy as my strong, silent father. My memories of him generate warmth. Never for a second did I feel I was not his daughter. He was pa to me and always will be. I heard from my mother that he was born a Hindu, but Albert Sherman and my grandfather enforced his change to Christianity. He embraced everything that was expected of him when he married my mother, Milly. His family never visited, and I suspect his change of faith could have been the reason. All paths are righteous. If one does not harm another living soul and the natural world, why should a change in faith be judged? My pa must have been a virtuous Hindu, because he certainly was a good Christian. He went to church every Sunday, treated us with kindness and had a reverence for the natural world. The plantation, much as I did not enjoy living there, instilled his respect for nature. I knew pa Chiddy loved my mother in his silent devotion—never questioning, never uttering a harsh word. To me, he was a spirit from another world. I could count on him to calm my mother when my teen headstrong attitude got under her skin.

I am relieved to know my true origins, but overcome with sadness that my wonderful mother endured much because of me. Yet she held onto her dignity, although her heart ached for Thomas...my father. I console myself that I am a part of him, and blessed to have had her present in my growing up days. That is the joy that sustains me, perhaps... that I might have brought her comfort in those aching years. She had an emptiness in her eyes when she thought no one was looking.

My bold and brazen attitude teased, 'Why are you

sad, ma? Have I upset you?' Her answer, as always, 'You could never make me sad, my eldest born, light of my life.' Then, I did not understand that I was a reminder, the constant candle to her lost love. She showered me with love, but never favoured me over my sister. We were loved equally by our parents. Pa Chiddy loved me, although by all calculations, he knew I was not his biological child. That was indisputable. I have no regrets. To be born out of love is a gift. My mother put family first. She honoured her parents in marrying pa Chiddy and prioritised me and Zola while remaining a caring wife to pa Chiddy. To know one is loved, is a primary human need. I am blessed to be living this with Aru. Our relationship is based on deep mutual love. Candace is my concern. I hope the love she gives is returned by the one who is deserving of her. As my mother lived for my happiness, so too I yearn for Candace's soulmate to come to her soon.

Once Zola, Candace, and I read and analysed my grandmother's journals and unleashed the dark past that returned like a haunting, I began cleaning my mother's home. Things fell apart in recent years when pa Chiddy, died. Zola was gracious in accepting that my biological father had bequeathed the plantation house to me. She gave me the space, alone in the house, with the ghosts I had to release.

'When you are ready, please call me to help you with cleaning the house. It's an enormous task to manage on your own. It might be good for us both to do this for ma. Ruth will be happy to assist, too. Norah's and Edgar's bond with ma lives through their family.'

'Thank you, Zola, for your patience and understanding. I am so grateful to you. I will ask you and Ruth to help me once I have processed all that has transpired. This alone time in the house will be healing for me.'

Her quiet smile left me to do what I had to do—make peace with my mother for never telling me who my real father was.

I started with my mother's bedroom. She enjoyed poetry and would quote lines to Zola and me when she was in a joyous mood. A brand new collection of Emily Dickinson's poems caught my eye. One page was dog-eared, and two circled lines in *Mine*, read, 'Mine, by the grave's repeal,' and 'Mine, while the ages steal!' In these lines, my mother found her freedom to celebrate, and not tarnish her only love. I lay on her bed trying to imagine what her life must have been like, with Thomas on the other side of the plantation. A field between them. I was much too wild a character to endure what she did. Sneaking out for more stolen moments with my love would have put me in dire straits with the law. Her only way of being with Thomas as man and wife would have been to leave the country. Race divided and forced the separation of their love.

I shuffled through her bedside drawer and found an empty pack of blood pressure pills, prescribed a week before she died. My heart somersaulted. A month's supply, with three weeks to go as per the date supplied—the box was bare!

Did she take all the pills to end her life?

My head spun as thought after thought raced through my mind, leaving me in a black hole of confusion. Why did she do it? Why did the hospital hide this from us? I lay back on her bed, covered my face with her pillow, and inhaled her sweet floral scent. Was this another dark secret that only I knew? Every fibre of my being told me I had to speak to the doctor who pronounced her dead. Her death certificate stated the cause of death as myocardial infarction. Had she concealed her health matters from us?

Her doctor declared, with a steady stony gaze, that old age caused her elevated blood pressure. I told him about the empty pill box. His response left me petrified.

'Let it be. You have cremated your mother. There was nothing untoward about her death. She collapsed outside the post office, and that is all there is to it.'

His stony eyes commanded my exit from his rooms. He left me no hope of knowing the truth. I dared not tell Zola, Candace, and Aru about my suspicions. They would probably say the doctor was right. My mental state would take precedence in all they said after the life-changing news I had to digest about my biological father and my mother's sudden death. Beneath this, my guilt for asking my mother to open her life to expose our family history seared in my veins. Am I a terrible daughter for wanting to bring clarity to my daughter's crumbling relationship?

Everything was because of my birth.

My mind could not distinguish what was worse. My existence or the blood-curdling secrets in our family.

For the first time in my life, I had to curb my tongue. Something I never did before. As my mother's loud and reckless daughter, I had to let ma have her dignity. She fought long and hard, in silence, to preserve it. Someday, Candace would do the same for me. Who knows what else may crawl out of my past? I was wild, after all.

My dearest ma, born on the wrong side of the colour line, dismissed as a statistic: *died of old age!*

Here I am now, the keeper of the final plantation secret. That's if it is as I perceive the end of my beloved ma's life.

I ARRIVED in Sydney two days before Candace returned to work. It was time for her to socialise with her peers. Isolation breeds misery. Too much came crashing down on her. Her mental wellness needed urgent prioritisation. I was anxious when her divorce was being processed, but Terence delivered by not forcing her hand for a DNA test. It had to be guilt that halted that request after Candace's and Jadon's trauma at the hands of his girlfriend. Perhaps he had a hidden good bone in him. The greater surprise was his acceptance that he would only have visitation rights on Candace's terms. She asked that either she or I be present when he wanted to see Jadon. Why he bothered to ask for this is something I'm still trying to understand. He was hellbent on abandoning his child.

There was no way he was going to toss aside my daughter and grandson. Never. If he thought ma Sugar was a sweet old mother-in-law, he was so wrong!

Terence destroyed his marriage, and Candace had a depth of strength he did not see coming. Some of the old Sugar-gal rubbed off on her. The audacity of the man to ask if they could patch up their rift like it was a tiny argument over nothing. Candace was done with being Mrs Laws! I had to break my family's silence for him, and she believed it took its toll on her grandma Milly.

I know what I know, but I cannot tell her what I know about her much adored grandmother.

This makes me complicit in our family's shadowed lives.

Candace loved Terence, but becoming a mother was her suit of armour. Her baby did not deserve nor need a chameleon father. We spent many hours chatting about life's challenges and the value of not reacting in the heat. Candace knew that love made her blind to Terence's flaws.

'I had to have this experience at this point in my life to awaken and sharpen my power of observation and survival skills.'

She rattled on without self-pity.

'Don't look worried, ma. I don't think the universe is punishing me. To be honest, I don't hate Terence. I just don't trust him anymore. Life will serve him whatever lesson he needs.'

My heart heaved with a mother's pain for her child, but my lips echoed strength.

'Oh Candace, you are so wise and level-headed, and I never praised you for your courage before this moment. Grandma Milly and I were anxious when you made your solo move to Australia, but you had much to teach us.'

She threw her head back and curled her legs up on the couch and laughed like a schoolgirl.

'I'm no saint. Don't canonise me just yet. I have a lot to learn from the errors I'm sure I will make in this life. Self-reflection is the gift I'm grateful to have gained. I get that from you, and you don't realise you have it!'

I answered my heart, 'You will find love again, darling, I'm certain. As for my self-reflection, I don't know. Remember, I was a headstrong young woman.'

'I'm not looking, wanting, or needing a man. Jadon is my love.'

'But allow yourself to be open to the possibility...'

Her glare stopped me from overstepping my maternal concern. In Sugar form, she told me where to get off!

'No, ma! No more. My work, Jadon, you, pa, and aunt Zola are my world. Let it be.'

My heart stormed, but I swallowed the urge to have a mother-daughter lecture. My silenced voice needed to say, 'What about you? You need a life.'

It was as though Candace read my thoughts.

'I'm happy. Whatever will be will be. Your blood flows in my veins. I have the grit I need to survive.'

On that note, we retired for the night. I wanted to tell Candace I had many questions for Terence. He was not free of me, just yet! He accepted I would be present during some of his visits to see Jadon, and I had every intention of letting him know the pain he caused my small family.

Nobody should get away with abusing the purest form of abundant love poured over them. Aru felt Candace's pain but contained his emotions. I was part Albert Sherman. I took nothing without a fight. If my daughter thought I had the gift of self-reflection, I did, for *my* family. Terence had better watch himself. A mother's pain for what her child endures at the senseless hands of another is a dangerous thing. I had every intention of making him squirm!

My conversation with Candace kept me up,

reigniting a memory I must have buried. I had to tell her before it slipped into oblivion.

It was the night uncle George came over to see my mother. While Jadon slept in the early hours of the morning, I met Candace in the kitchen for a cup of coffee.

'I hope you slept well because I didn't. This recollection is begging for your ears.'

'Our family is a layered onion, for sure. Begin, leave out nothing. I'm listening.' Candace winked.

'As you know, uncle George was never close to grandma Milly, so fifteen-year-old me was curious about his rare visit.'

'Yes, keep going. I want this in one sweep before Jadon wakes up. You deliberate and digress.'

Her forthright manner came as a sudden shock, but I knew she meant no unkindness.

'Uncle George met a fellow in the pub, or rather at the local shebeen, and he asked after my grandfather.'

'Throwback! You never mentioned this when we were with aunt Zola, sharing memories. Now, I'm burning to know what this is all about!'

'It surfaced during the night, perhaps because it disturbed me.'

'Who was the fellow he met? Not a long-lost relative?'

'Here's the thing. He said he was born in the same village grandpa Arnold hailed from, and that he was my grandpa's friend's son. No relative in the woodwork!'

'I hoped we had found some family in a secret vault!'

'Grandpa Arnold made sure no vault was unlocked. Anyway, the fellow said my grandpa had a wife and children that he left behind when he eloped with grandma Romola.'

'What? Another branch to the family?'

'Who knows? Uncle George said he bashed the man for lying and left the shebeen.'

'Please don't tell me that's it! We need to know if we have this other family.'

'I'm not going near that! I don't need long-lost relatives riddled with problems. My mother told him to leave it alone.'

'There are half-cousins a world away, or perhaps right here in this country and you are not curious to know who they are?'

'Remember, I heard that when I was fifteen, and anyway, I'm happy with our small family.'

'I have spent my entire life dreaming about finding a large extended family, and all I want for Jadon, is to tell him he has a big family. It's hard enough being an only child, you know.'

'I know you wanted siblings, but it was not possible for me. You will have more children, so Jadon does not have to know about grandpa Arnold's sordid past. What an irresponsible man, leaving a wife and children behind to start a new life. I don't think grandma Romola knew this.'

'More children? How? I don't think so. I was the only child in school who had nothing to share with having family overseas, and stories to tell.'

Candace walked around the kitchen, muttering to herself, and shaking her head.

'How are you not curious about this? You straddle two cultures, races, and you don't want to know more?'

'I do not want to know about life before grandma Romola. I am my mother's daughter and that is enough for me. There is so much history in that.'

I was determined to step out of the secret shadows of a past not worth memorialising.

The shedding of blood was not part of my life. Love mattered.

I flinched, hating that I brought this forgotten memory to the light. It sparked a need in Candace, and she would not let this bit of family history slip away.

As I grow older, I choose the moments I want to embrace, and the people I want in my corner. Candace wanted to create a family background for Jadon. We had to keep this part of our family background that my uncle George brought to my mother out of the light. Jadon did not need to know the untamed ways of his great-great-grandfather. He had no greatness to share.

When Zola called me to say we received a letter from Thomas Sherman's lawyer requesting we contact the office, my reaction was, 'Now, what family shadow needs light?'

'I don't think it's anything serious, but I could call and ask the reason for their communication. The letter is addressed to just you and me, under the heading, *For Milly's daughters*.'

'I'm intrigued and concerned, you should contact the office.'

When Zola told me we were required to pick up a box from Philip Jacobsen's office, I felt agitated that there might be more to my background. I was happy with the way things were. How long had this mystery box waited? It was left with the explicit instruction that it was to be handed to Milly's daughters upon her passing.

Candace urged me to return to South Africa to collect the box with Zola. Aru was due to arrive in Sydney in two weeks to spend three months with our grandson.

'I could ask the lawyer's office to keep the box until I returned in three months.'

'Ma, we both know whatever is in the box will agitate you and will ruin pa's time here. Ask aunt Zola if the office will accept a certified letter from you for her to collect the box because you are overseas.'

'That might be the best way, and perhaps your pa can bring the box over with him.'

'We don't know how big it is. It might be worth knowing that before you ask pa to bring it to you. Aunt

Zola should come with pa to look through the contents of the box with us.'

'We could ask her, but who knows if she will be keen to come out?'

'Let's leave that up to the gods.'

'My goodness, I've never heard you speak like that before. I'm praying for patience that I do not put too much pressure on Zola. If there's one thing I understand about myself, it is that I've always wanted things my way. It has been my downfall, but I am working on it.'

'My dear ma, you have mellowed so much since grandma Milly passed. I daresay I might miss my feisty mother.'

'With all your dear grandmother had to endure, I have nothing to complain about. I've not walked a step in her shoes.'

We both slumped into silence, reliving the revelations that came at us in my mother's and grandmother's painful cathartic unloading.

Much to my surprise, Zola needed no cajoling on coming to Sydney with Aru and the box of shadows. She refused to open the box until she was with me.

And so, the box made its way across the ocean down to Australia.

I met Aru and Zola at the airport, noting that the much awaited box was a medium size file box with the label, *For Milly*. Then another line under it read, *For Milly's daughters.*

We waited until morning after Aru and Zola had rested.

'Our family sure knows how to feed the suspense,' Candace laughed, 'a few hours more I will endure.'

'You were a curious child, and Christmas was not Christmas without you sneaking up to the tree and carefully pulling out the sticky tape to have a peek at your gift. We knew you did and none of us said anything.'

'And here I was all these years thinking I went undetected. That's a story Jadon is going to enjoy in a few years.'

Having my family under one roof again meant the world to me, but I had a restless night knowing that the box on the lounge table held our secret shadows.

I WAS up with the larks and brewing a pot of coffee when Aru touched my shoulder, making me jump out of my skin.

'Dear me, you are skittish. By now, you should be strong enough to accept anything that arrives from the past.'

'I did not hear you come in. Yeah, I thought I was strong, but you better accept this girl is getting old, and her former resolve is crumbling. More surprises will unnerve me.'

'Hurry with that coffee. You need it. Candace and

Zola are up and will be down shortly. I'm taking my coffee with me and will look after Jadon while you ladies delve into the past.'

'Thank you for helping with Jadon. I'll fill you in on what the box holds.'

'My grandson will always have my help as long as I have breath.' He threw me a parting shot, his eyes aglow with love.

Zola looked fresh, showered and dressed, while Candace and I sat around in our nightwear sipping coffee. Zola suggested I should open the box.

At the top of a bundle of papers was an envelope addressed to *Milly*.

'I don't feel right opening this. Why was it not given to my mother?'

'As our mother's eldest daughter, we expect you to open it and read it to us. That will make it a shared experience.'

'A shared shock, you mean?'

'Come on, quit the negativity, ma. Just open it!'

And open it I did...

The envelope sitting at the top of the open box read:

For you, Milly, from Edgar

I looked at Candace and Zola. Both leaned forward, staring at me.

'I can't believe that Edgar left this for ma. They shared a close bond, but I do not know what he left to her that sadly, she did not get to read.'

'Please get on with the task aunt Zola assigned you, ma. Your nervousness is making you garrulous, and me nervous.'

'Yes, begin reading what's inside that envelope.'

With both my daughter and sister agitated, I had to do what had to be done. The page inside the envelope was crafted with a stylus in a beautiful curly font.

Dear Milly,

I left this letter and box with Master Thomas' lawyer the day I brought his letter to you. I'm sorry I too must speak from my grave on matters that are private to you. You have been the secret daughter of my heart. My Siya loved you like a sister. We have much shared history between us. Over the years, I watched you grow into a kind young woman, but did not expect the fate that you would live through. But, dear Milly, rest knowing that to love and be loved is the bounteous blessing of our Lord.

I hope your life was not too difficult and know that Mr Chiddy was the right person for you at the right time. Your mother had a good heart and a clever head on her shoulders. You were the light that arrived in Mrs Romola's life.

I gathered all your crumpled writings from your bedroom bin to save you from detection by your father and brothers. Your secret remained as mine alone. I have preserved your writings, your poetry, and your discarded letters to Master Thomas, hoping it would bring you some joy in the later years. I added in a provision that, should this not reach you, then your daughters are to have the box.

They must know how special their mother is, the pain you bore, always with a smile for them.

May this bring naught but pleasure to you and your daughters.

Forever your servant in the Lord,

Edgar

We digested the power and beauty of Edgar's words. He was indeed a man like no other. Our moist eyes spoke of our healing that we knew would come once we read through the deepest part of our young mother's soul.

'I don't know how you both feel after this, but I prefer to leave grandma Milly's private words to another day. Edgar's letter has filled my emotional cup for today,' Candace whispered with her eyes closed.

'I agree. How about you, Sugar?'

'I'm with you both on that. Aru will be disappointed, he thought he had the day with Jadon.'

'Let him have another hour. I'll make a pot of tea and we can debrief.'

'Tea is a great idea. It was grandma Milly's elixir for all headaches and heartaches.'

'That headache heartache combination speaks of my life with Terence, although now he is just a headache.'

Zola laughed at Candace's pragmatic attitude.

'You're a chip off the old block, ma would have celebrated your strength,' Zola grinned.

'Well, we are of Indian stock, so tea is our mainstay.' I added.

Candace chirped, 'Look who's talking, multicultural mama!'

'Tea is in my blood. My mother made sure of that. Make sure Jadon loves it as much as we do.'

'It's a huge coffee drinking culture here, I don't know if tea will be his liquid gold.'

'Mothers have their secret way of inculcating tastes!' Zola piped in.

We lightened what we expected awaited us in Edgar's box. That could wait another day. If Aru had things to do, Jadon could join the ladies in his great grandmother's revelation of her secret shadowed past. Family history is important, and ours had much to pass down to the next generation. Good. Bad. Ugly. Truths had to be acknowledged, although the gory bits I would rather bury forever. Each one of us had to accept the past in our own way.

Rain arrived during the night, making me restless. I stepped out of bed and tip-toed downstairs to the kitchen for a drink of water. Palm trees in Candace's neighbour's backyard cast long eerie shadows swaying, bending low as though searching for something. Stolen sleep was my lifelong reaction to tension. I had to face whatever was in Edgar's box. An uneasiness crept through my body. A cup of tea would steady my nerves. I moved around the dark kitchen, catching my breath with each flash of lightning.

'Sugar, why are you up at this hour?'

I dropped behind the kitchen counter, my heart pulsated in tribal war drumbeats. It was Aru. Poor man was beside himself thinking I had fainted. He stroked my head and lifted me to my feet.

'Get some rest. Whatever is in that box has passed. It cannot hurt anything in your life. I know how strong you are. Believe that.'

'Oh, Aru, I don't know why I'm tense about the box that travelled across the ocean to me.'

'You and I know Edgar would hurt no one in your family, more particularly Milly's daughters, with whatever he felt you should know and have.'

'You're right, Aru. I'm letting my mind and emotions do a wild, uncontrollable dance.'

'Control it, you can do that. Bring your tea to bed. The storm feels sinister here, but it will pass.'

Aru's wise words and gentle arm around me, eased my anxiety. Although sleep evaded me, I was calm as thoughts of my mother slipped in and out of consciousness.

Did she know life as I know it? Did she feel loved, as I do with Aru and Candace? Was I a good daughter? I needed answers to understand a part, a major part, of my mother that remained in the shadows.

I was a mess the next morning, sighing, tidying up a tidy kitchen, rearranging the chairs in the lounge room, fluffing cushions that were bought a few days ago. Candace took control—no questions asked. The bags under my eyes, a dead giveaway that I was anxious.

Zola's silence was comforting, and Aru's presence as Candace opened the box calmed me. The rain had not let up and Jadon slept like a lambkin on cooler days. My family was around me, and we were embarking together into information on my mother from a different perspective. A trusted perspective. That held a level of solace, but Edgar never glossed over things he was passionate about. That worried me.

Truth is something we desire and fear.

A large pot of coffee, to keep me alert, and a packet of Tennis biscuits that Zola brought from South Africa would have to sustain us that morning. Candace held up an envelope marked *One.*

'Edgar was quite an organised and meticulous man. He marked everything in numerical order, so that is how we will read through the contents of his box.'

Zola and I agreed.

Edgar had flattened my mother's crumpled papers carrying unfinished lines that held her secrets and shadows. The lines that brought me close to tears read: *Will I ever be this happy, this loved again? I fear that which feels so right will never truly be mine...'*

There were long pauses between each unfolded paper, fading ink, and some indiscernible lines. I refilled the bottomless coffee pot each time my emotions surged.

Aru stepped in and out of the room to feed, calm, or change Jadon. With each reading, some longer than others, I felt immense gratitude for Aru. He was still with me at this stage of my life. I was first in his life, but slipped a notch when Candace was born. We had no secrets between us. Our lives were open to scrutiny from each other, with the promise that neither of us would be offended with suggestions for improvement. Perhaps that's why we are still as one. My birth was the only secret—we both learned this truth in the same moment. I admit I did not tell him about my brief relationship with Richard. That is a shadow I must bring to the light for him.

Candace called for a break and a regroup at 2 pm. Aru ordered a pizza lunch, knowing that nobody felt inclined to cook a meal.

I pondered on the reason why Edgar asked us, Milly's daughters, to collect his box from my father's attorney. I understood he wanted me to know my parents conceived me in the purity of their love. From the grave, he spoke to me through my mother's words. Healing comes from knowing the truth, and Edgar, wise Edgar, cast a light on my mother. He inched her out of the shadows with each note he included in his truth box.

We retreated to our private corners, not wanting to discuss the weight we felt and released. When we reconvened, my mother's journal, covered with gold paper, now fading in parts, beckoned to be opened. The first in ornate lettering read, *Mother, My Ma.*

MA IS A WONDERFUL WOMAN. She kept her own counsel, but never failed to provide for us, her family.

Zola and I stole a side glance at each other when Candace read the line:

I heard firsthand of an incident in my ma's life...

She struggled in her past life in her motherland, and here at the hands of my father. He silenced her with his lack of acknowledgement. He walked around her like she was dead. She walked around him, afraid of her footsteps. Her heart longed to return to her mother, but shame kept her in her life of suffering with the man who ripped her from her mother's womb. Not a woman yet, with child, she sailed the arduous journey to the land of false promises. The land that kept her imprisoned. She told me once I was her reason for living, that a daughter was a divine gift. The brimming tears which she held back from rolling down her cheeks made my innocent eyes cry for her. We had fleeting conversations when my father and brothers were out. Talking as mother and daughter was condemned as wasting useful time that could be used on domestic chores. Her voice was soft and tremulous in those sparse moments when she spoke, and she ended with, 'Do not tell your father and brothers that we spoke.'

What we did not expect was a pointy arrow right

through our hearts. This was a much later entry in my mother's journal.

My father was not a good man, but he was a monster when my beloved ma told me he destroyed her dignity. One night he returned home, drunk as usual, with an unknown man he invited into our home. He shoved my frightened ma into their bedroom with the drunk stranger, and locked the door. Her protests went unheard. My brothers did not save her from this abomination, and I did not hear her cries. After that horrid night, she stayed in her room for a week, groaning, praying, creeping out in the dead of night to wash herself. I knocked on her door one night when we were the only two in the house and asked her if I could come in. She protested, telling me to remain in my room, and finally she let me in when I sat sobbing at her door.

Her face was bruised, her lips pale and cracked.

She said she was sick, and I was not to sit in her room for too long to avoid catching what she had. I made her a cup of tea and left her to sleep as she instructed, and again she said, 'Do not tell your father and brothers that we spoke.'

Her voice was faint, and eyes filled with fear. Those words gave us our sacred space.

It was only when she told me I should marry Chiddy because he was a good man that she told me about my father's treacherous treatment of her. He passed her off as payment for his gambling debt to a drunken white man. He used her to free himself from a beating he deserved. Which man does such a thing? I am ashamed to think that such a man is my father. As I write this, I feel anger, repulsion, and sadness for what my silent mother endured. Her trauma became her mission to find me a good man. She never spoke of Thomas nor my hidden, bulging belly. Her focus was on marrying me off to a good man to avoid what my father would do to us.

We paused. Candace stood up and paced the floor like an enraged lion in an enclosure. Zola, dabbed her eyes, holding back the sobs heaving in her chest.

'What men did we have in our family? How could they allow this abuse?' Candace exploded, and Jadon cried when he heard his mother's raised voice.

We acknowledged what my grandmother endured was worse than death. My darling ma was her only compassionate ear for her woes, the only one she opened her truth to, knowing she could trust her daughter.

'Yes, marriage in that generation came with its own brand of male superiority.'

Candace walked up to me still raging, anger mixed with tears.

'That generation! I'm sorry, in every generation women need to scrutinise who they trust, or marry! Here's living proof of this, ma! You won the lottery with pa, but your marriage did not break this horrible cycle I'm facing today. Aunt Zola is the wisest of us all, hence her inner peace.'

Zola's shadowed smile left us none the wiser on whether she knew love and lost it. I knew nothing about it. As pa Chiddy's daughter, or our grandmother's granddaughter and mother's daughter, Zola kept her own counsel on matters of her heart.

'I agree the two generations of women before us had no voice. The fear of poverty estranged them from their cultural communities. They lacked generational self-confidence. We must be grateful for where we are now in our lives and pay homage to our ancestors.'

'Yes, but it angers me that family can turn their backs on something as horrible as what happened to great-grandmother Romola.'

No words could erase the horror she endured.

'Surely, there can't be anything worse in ma's journals, after this...' Zola whispered with downcast eyes.

A series of random entries, undated, spoke of uprisings on some plantations, and secret meetings that made her fearful for my father, Thomas' safety. We spent two more days perusing through my ma's words. The rawness of her emotions conveyed in her own words had a strange way of healing us. Her writing was as she spoke, but without her usual reservation. She was free to reveal her inner self, free from judgement. In that I found my lesson. Who was I to mistreat Terence? He was Jadon's father, and someday the boy will acknowledge his father and his family. The last thing I would want is for him to find out, after I have passed, when I cannot defend myself, that I put his father through the ringer for questioning his birth. That was Candace's prerogative.

The past gets convoluted when it's left in the hands of the wrong teller. I received the truth from trusted sources and left it at that. My affair with Richard was the truth that Aru deserved. It was before his time, but to rest easy, I must tell him. Forgiveness is the salt in any relationship, but sometimes, as in Candace's case, one must forgive and move on. I am inclined to say move away, but Jadon ties her to Terence. Aru gave me a refreshed perspective when he said I had to understand as much as we lived with the shadows of segregation, Terence and his family lived through the harshest racial prejudice in a unique system. His grandmother's probing into our family's white ancestry came from her own fear and hardship. She was looking out for her grandson. While I accepted what he said, I was looking out for my grandson, too.

Terence had a lifetime ahead of him to get rid of the doubt that festered. He almost lost his child in a frightful twist of events that he invited. He would have more hurdles yet to come, so who was I to add another?

———

WHEN ZOLA RECEIVED news from a friend that George had passed, her immediate reaction was to return to South Africa for his last rites. My anger for what my mother and grandmother endured, because he allowed it to continue, made me reluctant to return. Candace advised I should accompany Zola to lay him to rest. My wise daughter said it would help to put my demons to rest. And so it was to be. Zola and I laid our uncle George in the grave next to my grandfather.

This was the end of the known male line on my mother's side of the family. There was an uncanny sense of relief in acknowledging that reality— the last warrior was put to rest. This finality forced me to look ahead. A week after uncle George's burial, I returned to Sydney. Zola took care of his affairs and promised to return for a visit in two months. It would be longer. Winding up the estate of the deceased came with its own set of complications. Zola was a loner, much like uncle James. She inherited her complexity from pa Chiddy and growing up around our uncle James. He never returned to the family fold, and I feared losing my sister this way. I had to allow Zola to fulfil her duty to uncle George, but had to ensure she did not fade into her own world without us. My bitterness for the mistreatment of two generations of women, the two we held closely, had to dissolve.

I believe it will as I grow in the acceptance that while time and place determine the level of freedom one has in the choices made, we must first accept that pain or suffering is the path to recovery.

I stand on the border of time—my mother's life to my right, imprinting my identity—to my left, the life Candace and Jadon are yet to live, in the shadows behind me, the ancestral family tree with many bare branches. Ahead, my time with Aru and Zola as our golden years advance.

NO LIFE LIVED IS PERFECT, we make the most of what we have inherited, and move on.

It is easier to build strong children than to repair broken men.

— Frederick Douglass

AFTERWORD

Writing a fictional recollection of events on the lives of an indentured family on the sugar fields of Natal, South Africa, stems from a longheld desire to create my version of life then.

Personal and cultural pasts are threatened when people flee their motherland because of war, poverty, or to escape something sinister—all in a quest for a better life. Whatever the reason, the flight is the fight for expected renewed self-definition, anchored to the promise of success in a different place. Nobody serves a good life on a platter. It must be earned through hard work, and commitment, if success is the desired fruit. Deception dishes up abundant enticement in the language of a grand feast when recruiting hunger.

It is up to the individual to use the opportunity, if one dares call it that, to create a better life.

Indentured sugar field labourers, seduced by the promise of colonisation, faced a loss of culture, identity, and fragmentation of family. In constructing this historical fiction/family drama, the historical details do not surpass the dominant fictional aspect of the novel—characters' angst and joy in life's journey. Fictional characters and situations arise against the backdrop of the historical details affecting the lives of indentured labourers and their families in South Africa, alongside the swell of an advancing apartheid mindset that ate into the spirit of all its people.

The escalation of the desire for success among the indentured labour cohort, sourced from the Indian continent, unnerved colonialists who promoted their return passage after the indenture period. Some took up the offer while the vast majority opted to remain in South Africa.

This expansive diaspora resulted in South Africa being a country boasting the second largest Indian population outside India. Over time, the offspring of indentured labourers held various occupations, from business owners, health care professionals, teachers, academics, accountants, legal professionals, and many more. The fervent desire for education led to the creation of schools within racially segregated residential zoning, and mammoth advancement followed through each successive generation.

Colonialism entrenched mind, manners and morals until Authenticity raised her hand saying, 'I will be ME!'

Also by Mala Naidoo

Novels:

Across Time and Space

Vindication Across Time

Souls of Her Daughters

Chosen Lives

What Change May Come

Aurora Days

Gallery Nights

Blackwater Mornings

Short Stories:

The Rain

Life's Seasons

Crossings

Poetry:

Random Heart Poetry : Light and Shade

Random Heart Poetry : Visions and Voices

Random Heart Poetry : Time and Place

Random Heart Poetry : Rainbows and Shards

SIGN UP FOR MORE!

Thank you for reading *Plantation Shadows*.

Sign up to my website www.malanaidoo.com for FREE short stories and seasonal gift stories.

Best wishes,

Mala Naidoo